A ZEBRA REGENCY ROMANCE

The Candlelight Wish

Janice Bennett

*A fairy godmother meets
a most unwilling
Cinderella....*

ZEBRA/0-8217-6263-X
(CANADA $6.50) U.S. $4.99

D0030076

ISBN 0-8217-6263-X

9 780821 762639

50499

WALTZES AND WISHES

Phoebe had been hearing the melodic notes of the flute and violin since they had come outside. Now they broke into a familiar waltz melody. She caught herself humming it, and when Miles stood and held out his hand to her, it seemed the most natural thing in the world to take it.

Lucilla had a point, Phoebe reflected as she looked up at Miles, aware of the play of shadow and moonlight on the planes and angles of his face. A touch of romance added to one's existence, gave one's heart a reason to beat faster, one's breath to come more quickly, one's flesh to tingle with the contact. She allowed the music to flow over and through her, breathed in the sweet scents of the garden. Awareness swept over her, of his eyes, his smile, of the tangible bond that seemed to link them as surely as did his touch. When he gathered her in his arms for the circling steps, she melted against him, losing herself in the overwhelming sensations he created in her. He released her all too soon into the open movements, then pulled her close once more. And all the while his hand warmed hers in a clasp so perfect it seemed impossible to break it.

The music ended, and from within the house came the sound of voices. For a long moment they stood together, their hands still touching. Then he led her back to the bench and settled at her side, his gaze still holding hers. Slowly, he lifted one finger to touch her cheek, then brush tendrils of hair back from her face.

In another moment, the hazy thought filtered into Phoebe's mind that he might kiss her. . . .

Books by Janice Bennett

REGENCIES

AN ELIGIBLE BRIDE
TANGLED WEB
MIDNIGHT MASQUE
AN INTRIGUING DESIRE
A TEMPTING MISS
A LOGICAL LADY
A LADY'S CHAMPION
THE MATCHMAKING GHOST
THE CANDLELIGHT WISH

REGENCY MYSTERIES

A MYSTERIOUS MISS
A DANGEROUS INTRIGUE
A DESPERATE GAMBLE

TIME TRAVELS

A TIMELY AFFAIR
FOREVER IN TIME
A CHRISTMAS KEEPSAKE
A TOUCH OF FOREVER
ACROSS FOREVER

FUTURISTIC

AMETHYST MOON

Published by Zebra Books and Pinnacle

THE
CANDLELIGHT
WISH

Janice Bennett

Zebra Books
Kensington Publishing Corp.
http://www.zebrabooks.com

ZEBRA BOOKS are published by

Kensington Publishing Corp.
850 Third Avenue
New York, NY 10022

First Printing: July, 1999
10 9 8 7 6 5 4 3 2 1

Printed in the United States of America

For John, for his patience. Thank you.

Prologue

The water in the shallow silver basin shimmered with more than the reflection of the sunlight that filtered through the lace curtains. Without so much as a breath of air to aid it, the surface rippled, setting colors swirling in the mirrored interior. Images took tentative form, shifted to an indeterminate blur, then went shooting and sparkling across the wide surface.

Beside the lace-covered sideboard on which the basin rested, a long-haired white cat of comfortable proportions sprawled lazily on the windowsill enjoying the morning's warmth. The tip of his tail twitched as if some dream disturbed his slumbers. He blinked sleepy eyes, yawned cavernously, and uncurled his considerable length to stretch with the concentration only a feline could give to such an occupation. He settled on his haunches, and his thick tail wrapped about his feet.

The ripples continued in the basin, catching the cat's attention. He cocked his head, and his large green eyes narrowed. He hunkered down and crept forward, one cautious step at a time, until he peered into the glittering waters. Candles seemed to glow within, filling the mirrored interior with magical, dancing flames.

For a long moment, the cat considered this spectacle. Then his tail twitched, and he sprang from the sideboard to the polished plank floor. With a grace amazing in an animal of such girth, he bounded through the open doorway, down the short hall, across the spacious kitchen and out into the garden.

Lilac bushes lined the cottage's stone walls, the huge blossoms making the air heavy with their sweet scent. Thyme and moss filled the gaps between the flagged paving stones which the cat sped across; for once, he didn't linger to sniff the patch of catnip planted especially for him, or to watch the butterflies that flitted among the roses. Across the vegetable garden he darted, to where a woman knelt amid the fragrant herbs.

She was of average height, her plump figure arrayed in a dark green tunic knotted about her waist with a golden cord. Gloves covered her hands as she leaned forward to pull a stubborn weed from amid the chamomile. Copious amounts of pale hair, mostly confined in braids, wound about her head and kept her wide-brimmed straw hat from fitting properly. One could easily mistake her for one's beloved aunt—if one's aunt was possessed of a reprehensible sense of humor and violet eyes full of mischief. She might have been any age from thirty to fifty, except that Xanthe existed outside of time as the majority of the world knew it. She had, in fact, tended this very same garden with loving delight for hundreds upon hundreds of years.

The cat slowed as he reached her, and positioned himself, true to his nature, in the midst of her work so she couldn't possibly continue, and meowed.

Xanthe sat back on her heels and regarded him with amused exasperation. "Well, Titus?"

For answer, he meowed again, the sound imperious and demanding.

Xanthe's eyebrows rose. "My basin? Candles? Did you see anyone?"

Again the cat meowed, but this time the very tone of it conveyed the negative.

"Well, I had better come at once, then, hadn't I?" She stripped off her gloves and laid them with her trowel, then hunched her shoulders to ease them from the stiffness of her labors. A double set of oval wings rose with them, the feathers almost transparent and tipped with gold. A single fluff of down drifted to the stones.

Xanthe stood, and her elegant wings spread to their full span of six feet, then refolded themselves neatly down her back. Fairy wings, not in the least angelic. More showy than useful, and she had to keep them invisible on her frequent visits to humans. Still, it felt good to allow them their natural freedom here, in the privacy of her own home.

Titus paced majestically before her, leading the way, keeping his steps just quick enough so Xanthe didn't trip over him. Time for that, later. He preceded her into the breakfast parlor, sprang onto the sideboard, and settled beside the basin, tail once more tightly wrapped about his feet. The water still rippled and shimmered, and the colors danced within the bowl.

"Candles," murmured Xanthe. She pulled open the top drawer of the chest and rummaged through an assortment of beeswax tapers, violet and pink, lemon and sky blue, mint green and orange and white. She located six of the latter, and set them in silver holders, chased with the same pattern of oak and holly leaves as the mirrored basin. When she had them arranged about the shimmering bowl, she lit them, passed her hands over the rippling waters, and sat down to wait, humming softly. Titus joined in, his encouraging purr rumbling deep in his throat as he regarded her workings with feline equanimity.

Almost at once, the water swelled as if with a tide, then roiled, transforming the images to a kaleidoscope of fractured colors. Xanthe passed her hand over the basin once more, still humming, and the waters quieted, then stilled. For perhaps five seconds the basin went opaque; then for a long moment it glowed with an inner fire. Then it cleared.

Distinctly, as if seen through a window, the face of a young lady appeared. A rather pretty face, oval and delicate, dominated by a pair of huge eyes the shade of sea-smoke, which gazed with wistful contemplation into the flame of a candle. A profuse amount of coppery brown curls clustered about her ears, falling from a knot on the top of her head. A small mole emphasized the corner of her full mouth. An earnest face, this fairy godchild of hers possessed, hiding a personality to be reckoned with.

Xanthe closed her eyes, attuning herself. Abruptly she frowned, wrinkling her nose, then as suddenly laughed. She turned to Titus, who regarded her with stoic patience. "Her name," she announced, "is Phoebe Caldicot."

Titus opened his mouth in a soundless meow, and the very tip of his tail twitched.

"No, she is confused. Her head and her heart, you know. The desires of one never seem to agree with the desires of the other. They so rarely do. It shall be a delight to help her sort it all out."

Titus made an inquisitive, stuttering sound.

"Not yet, but soon." She passed her hand over the basin once more, and the face shimmered, then ebbed away with the rippling of the water. Three full minutes passed, then stillness reigned once more. Only the brilliant sunlight glinted on the surface, fracturing and shooting sparkles of light about the room from the mirrored interior. Xanthe extinguished the tapers, then stepped back and looked at Titus. "Well?" she asked the cat. "Are you ready to go back to work?"

For answer, Titus blinked.

Xanthe nodded. "So am I." She strode from the room, bent on making her necessary preparations. A single gold-tipped, transparent feather fluttered to the floor behind her.

One

The chill breeze of the early April night whipped about Miss Phoebe Caldicot, tugging at the shawl she had cast about her shoulders. Next time, she fumed, she would wear a warmer one; but, then, she'd hardly expected to go out at such an hour. She'd dressed as usual, for an evening safe within the walls of the Misses Crippenham's Academy for Young Ladies, not for searching Sydney Gardens for an errant pupil.

She cast a fulminating glance at the young lady who hurried at her side, bundled in a warm cloak with its hood well up to cover her distinctive titian-colored hair. At least Miss Lucilla Saunderton showed some measure of discretion. Phoebe could only wish she had displayed it earlier and shrunk from this clandestine meeting with a half-pay officer she had met only the previous day. It had seemed harmless enough at the time to allow three of their young ladies to go shopping unsupervised in Milsom Street. She'd begun to guess her mistake upon their return, when she'd noted Lucilla's glowing, mischievous looks and heard the giggling of the other two girls. In the six years she'd been deportment and pianoforte instructress at the Academy, Phoebe had learned to tell the signs when one of the girls fancied herself in the throes of some romantic passion. And why could it not, just once, be with some respectable young gentleman? But no, the girls always seemed to feel compelled to slip away to meet their shockingly ineligible gallants in secret. Lucilla had proved no different.

If Phoebe hadn't wrenched the truth of the girl's whereabouts from her two closest friends, the consequences could well have been disastrous. As it was, Phoebe had no idea whether or not she could extricate them from this scandal undetected. Society did not take a kind view of such escapades on the part of a gently nurtured young lady of quality. The Misses Crippenham took an even dimmer one.

And as for the instructresses whose job it was to keep an eye on the girls—she quickened her pace. She could *not* afford to lose her job.

Lucilla peeped over at her. "It was not so very terrible," she ventured, the first words she had spoken since Phoebe had propelled her out of the Sydney Gardens some twenty minutes before. "He was truly the gentleman, and so terribly romantic. He likened my eyes to the fairy glow of the lanterns."

"There is nothing in the least bit romantic about ruining your reputation," Phoebe shot back.

"But I didn't!" cried the girl. "Miss Caldicot, truly I did not. No one recognized me. At least, I know we bumped into old Mrs. Brubaker, but she is so nearsighted she is almost blind. She could not possibly have known who I was."

"And what of Mr. Tallant?" Phoebe demanded. "He

is the most dreadful gossip, and if he realized who you were, the story will be all over Bath by morning."

"Bath!" Lucilla said the name witheringly. "I shall be off to London tomorrow, at last! They may say what they like in Bath."

"Your departure is by no means certain. And what is said in Bath is frequently repeated in London."

Lucilla halted, turning to face her instructress. "You are being unkind. And as for my departure, why else would my brother have come here, and called at the school at such a time of night instead of waiting until morning? Depend upon it, he *must* have found someone to chaperon me for the Season, and wanted me to pack upon the instant."

Phoebe took her by the arm and dragged her forward.

"If he learns where you really were tonight, he might change his mind."

"He would not!" And then, in a smaller voice, "What did you tell them when you found I was not in my room?"

"That I had forgotten you were visiting Miss Middleton. But, Lucy, I cannot convince myself that—"

"Georgeana Middleton?" Lucy Saunderton demanded with scorn in her voice. "Why ever should I wish to visit her? Even if she does live in that beautiful house with her great aunt. I should not like her any better if she lived in a palace!"

"She was the only one of the day students I could think of on the spur of the moment." And that was because she had only that afternoon set both Miss Middleton and Miss Saunderton to copying out letters as a punishment for arguing when they should have been attending to their lessons.

"Well, I should never have thought of *her*," muttered Lucilla, then added as they turned off Trim Street and into Barton, "London at last! Oh, Miss Caldicot, I can hardly believe it! If only my sister Juliana had not been in the family way, I should have been brought out already, during the Little Season, for I shall be eighteen in a few months, and that is quite old."

"Ancient," agreed Phoebe, a touch of her usual amusement returning to her. "Practically an ape leader. I wonder why you should even bother at such a late date."

Lucilla giggled. "I knew you could not really be angry with me, best and dearest of my teachers. It was only a lark, after all."

"A lark?" This time, it was Phoebe who halted, staring at her charge. "Stealing from your room when you were supposed to be in bed to keep a tryst with a man is a lark?"

"With a *gentleman*," Lucilla corrected. "An officer."

"Do you truly think that makes your conduct less reprehensible?" demanded Phoebe.

Lucilla's gaze dropped to the toes of her dainty slippers, and she started forward once more. "I did nothing so truly terrible." Her voice took on a sulky note.

"I see. Then you intend to tell your brother all about tonight's escapade?"

Lucilla spun to face her. "You—you will not tell him, will you? Oh, you couldn't be so cruel."

"Not after I was at such pains to convince everyone

at the school that you were with one of the other girls," Phoebe reminded her.

Lucilla groaned. "Georgeana Middleton will tell everyone she never saw me tonight. You may depend upon it!"

"Not," said Phoebe with a measure of satisfaction, "if she wishes me to remain quiet about a small indiscretion of her own."

Lucilla brightened. "No, really? What has she done, Miss Caldicot?"

"Have I ever told anyone about your escapades?" Phoebe demanded.

"No, *dearest* Miss Caldicot," came the subdued response. "And you know I am grateful."

"Then, I am hardly likely to reveal anyone else's, am I?"

Lucilla fell silent, and they turned into Queen's Square before she spoke again. "Do you know things about many of us?" she asked in a fascinated tone.

"Almost every single one of you," Phoebe averred, though without much truth. "Come, the street seems deserted," she added, casting a considering gaze up and down the quiet square.

To her relief, very few lights burned, and these stood at sufficient distance to make their own passing that of mere shadows. Phoebe propelled Lucilla across to the school, cast an assessing glance at the darkened upper-story windows, and nodded in satisfaction. The school slumbered in peace; they might well slip in undetected. She mounted the shallow steps and tried the door.

It wouldn't budge. In disbelief, she tried again. She

had left it on the latch to assure an easy return. She tried once more, not wanting to accept that someone doing the final rounds for the night had locked them out.

"Can we not get in?" Lucilla whispered, alarmed.

"Oh, we can get in. It will just be a bit more difficult than I had intended." Phoebe returned to the street, eyeing the entry with disapprobation, then with a sigh slipped down the area steps. But here, the door to the kitchens remained firmly barred against them, as well. Phoebe stepped back, eyeing the windows, considering.

Lucilla peered over her shoulder. "What are we to do?"

Phoebe led the way back to the street, then cast an uneasy glance around the square. Ridiculous, of course, yet she couldn't rid herself of the feeling someone lurked nearby, watching them. She shook off the sensation and turned her attention to the lower-floor windows. The second one over in the music room had a latch that tended to stick. It might not have locked properly. She clambered onto the iron railing, but a lady of her inadequate inches could not so much as touch the sill, even from this added height.

"We *must* get in," Lucy hissed. "Let me try."

"I wouldn't recommend it," drawled a deep, masculine voice from just behind them. "You are sure to fall, Lucy, and you could hardly make your curtsy to society with a sprained ankle."

Lucy jumped. "Miles! Where— What—" She broke off, staring aghast at her elder brother.

Phoebe, who still balanced precariously on the iron

railing, looked down in consternation upon the solid figure of a broad-shouldered gentleman of considerable height. In the darkness she could make out little of his features except for a pair of bright, penetrating eyes that held her within their spell. She swallowed and found herself breathless in a manner that had absolutely nothing to do with her current predicament.

"Miss Caldicot, I presume? May I assist you?" His voice sounded polite but aloof.

There was nothing aloof about his actions, though. Before Phoebe could respond, he reached out, caught her about her waist, and lifted her easily from her perch. Her weight troubled him not at all—which was no wonder, as insignificantly tiny as she was. Still, the strength of his hands, and the reassuring solidity of the chest against which she found herself pressed, sent an oddly pleasurable shiver through her.

He set her on her feet, and for a moment she experienced a sense of loss as he withdrew his support. Ridiculous, of course, but the sheer power of the man washed over her, making her vividly aware of his nearness.

His brow lowered in a frown, but before he could speak, Lucy broke in. "What are you doing here?" she wailed. "Oh, if it isn't just like you to appear just when—" She broke off.

"Just when you were getting into a scrape?" He made the question sound innocent.

"Oh, I hate you!" the girl cried.

"Of course you do," he soothed. "But I do not believe this is the place to tell me so in detail, do you? I know this may seem an outlandish suggestion," he added, turning back to Phoebe, "but you might find it much easier to enter if you simply apply the door knocker."

"No!" cried Lucy.

Phoebe eyed him with speculation. "A kind-hearted gentleman," she suggested, "might help us to gain entry without announcing it to the household."

"But I am not a kind-hearted gentleman. I am a brother—and a guardian." And with that, he mounted the steps and suited action to words.

Lucy cowered, and Phoebe glared at his back. A most unobliging brother, she fumed; but already the maid Sarah opened the door to them, and only one course presented itself to Phoebe. She swept up the stairs, pushing Lucy before her, then turned on the threshold and held out her hand to Lucy's brother. "I must thank you again for escorting us home, sir. Come, Lucilla, it is time and past you were in your bed. Good night, sir," she added over her shoulder.

"But we have not yet finished our discussion." Somehow, he stood in the darkened entry hall just behind her, the door firmly closed to the street.

"It is quite late," she protested, inserting a note of authority into her voice.

He ignored it. "I shall not keep you long. Is there an office we might use, or would you rather remain here?"

Here, where every girl in the school who chose to peer over the banister might listen in. She forced a smile to her lips. "The music room, perhaps?"

"Miss Caldicot," whispered Lucy, her voice strained, her expression one of extreme anxiety.

"Run along to bed, Lucilla. I feel certain your brother will call again tomorrow."

"You may depend upon that." He regarded Lucy with a creased brow.

The girl sniffed, cast one last appealing glance at Phoebe, then made her way up the stairs. Phoebe knew a temptation to follow her, but forced herself to light a taper from the single candle that burned in the hall, and crossed to the room where she had spent many an unpleasant afternoon with her music classes.

She lit the nearest candelabrum and heard the door close with a fatalistic thud. Well, she was for it now, she supposed. Gathering her courage, she turned to face him, and saw him clearly for the first time. He swept a shallow, curly beaver from his head, revealing a riot of thickly curling hair that in the indifferent light might have been any dark shade; it gleamed with mahogany highlights. Wide-set eyes studied her from above a nose with a decidedly aquiline cast, and a generous mouth curved upward in a cool, assessing smile that nevertheless turned her knees to jelly. If she were of the same nature as her romantically inclined pupils, he might set her heart fluttering. As it was, his effect on her bore a distinct resemblance to the time one of the younger girls had catapulted into her stomach. With an unusual measure of difficulty, she commanded her voice. "What is it you wished to say, sir?"

"It is Miss Caldicot, is it not?" The cordiality had left his tone, and the eyes that regarded her held a cold glint of steel. "I wish to be quite certain about that."

She inclined her head. Every instinct warned her to

be wary. He exuded an aura of power, of implacability, that challenged her own authority here, where he was the visitor and she at home and supposedly in charge. "And you are Sir Miles Saunderton?"

He, too, inclined his head. "Now that the niceties have been observed, you will oblige me by explaining where my sister went this night. And we shall save considerable time if you do not try to fob me off with that nonsense about Miss Middleton."

"She wished to attend the concert at Sydney Gardens, but the Misses Crippenham decided they would rather the girls not go."

"So my sister slipped out when she was thought to have gone to bed?"

Phoebe made no response.

"I see. You don't know. Did you find her alone?"

She raised a haughty eyebrow. "As you saw, none of our other young ladies went with her."

The creases in his brow deepened. "That is not what I asked, and well you know it. I cannot imagine even a young lady as flighty as my sister slipping out to a concert on a chill night merely for the novelty of it. She went to meet someone, did she not?"

Phoebe straightened to her full five feet and a hair. "I have no idea why she went. You shall have to ask her that, yourself."

"I intend to. But as her guardian, I believe I have the right to be informed of such matters by her instructresses."

He had, of course, but she didn't feel like admitting it.

"An officer, I presume. Foot or Hussar?" he asked.

She blinked. "How—?" she began, then broke off at the triumph in his expression, vexed with herself for giving that much away.

"I might have known. Where did she meet him? Or do you not know that, either?"

Phoebe stiffened. "I am sorry if we have not guarded your sister as well as you might like—"

"As well as I have the right to expect," he snapped back.

Her chin rose. "We are not accustomed to young ladies who must be kept under constant surveillance."

His eyes flashed with sudden anger. He opened his mouth, closed it again, then after a moment said, "I see there is no point in speaking with you any further."

"Indeed, there is not," she agreed with extreme cordiality.

"Then, I will wish you good night." He gave her a curt, dismissive nod and strode out.

She remained where she stood, fuming at the high-handed tone he had taken with her, at the sheer arrogance of the man. Obviously, he was too accustomed to having his own way, of having his every whim catered to. She would miss Lucilla Saunderton, of course, but the girl's absence from the Academy would be a small price to pay not to have that supercilious brother inflicted upon her again.

Then the probable consequences of this acrimonious interview dawned on her. He would lodge his complaint with the Misses Crippenham in the morning. Would they blame her for Lucilla's reprehensible behavior? Reasonably, they could not. But little of reason characterized those two ladies when the reputation of their academy lay at stake. She could only hope she would not become their burnt offering on the altar of respectability. If she were to lose her job— But that did not bear thinking about. She would not lose it. She *could* not.

Holding that thought in her mind, she extinguished the candles, then made her way up the several flights of stairs to the tiny apartment in the attics that was her room. Originally supplied with a narrow bedstead, a wardrobe, and a chest of drawers with a small mirror, Phoebe had added to it a padded chair, a small writing desk, and a bookcase crammed with her favorite volumes of poetry and literature. A colorful counterpane covered the bed, a rather fetching brass candelabrum she had purchased quite cheaply from a pawnbroker stood on the writing desk, and a bowl of dried flower petals rested on a tatted lace table scarf on the dresser, wafting a delicate scent throughout the chamber. More tatted lace covered the single window, and what little spare time Phoebe could muster, she devoted to making another piece to go under the candelabrum.

Home—at least until she could find some way to escape the drudgery of academy life. That wouldn't be for a while yet, not until Thomas graduated from Cambridge and joined the ranks of lowly curates. Even then, he would need some form of supplemental income until he was able to secure a vicarage with a comfortable living.

She picked up her young brother's latest letter, and found some solace in rereading the lines crossed so carefully to save her the expense of receiving a second sheet. His studies prospered—but then, they always did. In fact, only one of his many paragraphs disturbed her. It grieved him, he wrote, that he had yet to make the sort of connection that would assure him of a living when he graduated, so he would no longer be a burden to her.

Phoebe's fingers tightened on the page. He would meet someone, or obtain a recommendation, or discover a patron among the wealthy and influential gentlemen who maintained their old ties to their university. It might take time, of course—another month, perhaps another term—but he would manage it. He had to. In her own subservient position she had no chance of finding him a patron; she was lucky enough to be able to earn sufficient funds to help meet his expenses.

Of course, if she'd enjoyed a Season and been able to marry— But that had never been financially possible. Best to shove such a wistful dream to the back of her mind. She knew all too well that brooding over the impossible did no good. A suitable marriage, while it would solve so many of her difficulties, would not come her way. Setting aside Thomas's letter, she prepared for bed and slipped between the sheets.

Even without a patron, she and Thomas would manage, she assured herself as she slipped toward sleep. She had only to retain her position for two or three years more, at the most.

But she had to retain it. Both she and Thomas desperately needed the money she earned.

An image rose in her mind of Sir Miles Saunderton's tall, dynamic figure, of the implacability of his expression, and her heart shrank within her.

Phoebe entered the dining room a trifle late the following morning, to be met by a frown of disapproval from a gaunt lady of advancing years and receding patience. The spinster wore her usual high-necked gown of brown merino, made long in the sleeve, and the steely gray plaits of her hair wound about her head in a style that defied so much as a single tendril to dare to escape confinement. The irascible temperament of Miss Aurelia Crippenham, the junior of the sisters who ran the Academy, had never been known to improve one jot with the consumption of her breakfast.

Phoebe murmured an excuse, very much aware of the agonized gaze of Miss Lucilla Saunderton following her as she filled her plate and took her accustomed seat.

The elder Miss Crippenham, a softer, plumper version of her younger sister, appeared in the doorway. The gaze she cast about the assembled company held a resignation and regret, and more than a little annoyance. It settled on Lucilla. "Miss Saunderton," she said in a weary voice, "you will oblige me by coming to my office, if you please."

Phoebe looked up and met the unspoken plea for reassurance in Lucilla's eyes. She gave her a smile of encouragement, then resolutely studied her plate while the girl hurried from the room. Lucy had nothing to fear; her brother must have returned, and would shortly whisk her from the clutches of the martinets who ran the Academy, leaving Phoebe to bear the brunt of their annoyance. While Lucy set forth to enjoy an undoubtedly successful London Season, Phoebe would remain here, in deep disgrace, until some new problem redirected the attentions of the Misses Crippenham. Disgrace she could bear, as long as she retained her position—and her salary.

The meal continued in a silence unusually tense. Only an occasional whisper sounded, to be hushed when Miss Aurelia fixed the culprit with an icy stare. Phoebe kept an eye on the door, but Lucilla did not return. At last, as the hour neared for the first lessons of the day, she gathered her other students, shooed them up the stairs, and set them to their task.

A short while later, a sudden whispering and giggling erupted in the schoolroom that should have contained only the sounds of young ladies hard at work composing letters of acceptance and refusal to a variety of social engagements. Phoebe looked up from the poorly phrased example she corrected. Five of her six charges remained at their writing tables, but one had crept to the window which looked down on Queen's Square.

"He's stepping down," hissed Miss Georgeana Middleton, an enterprising sixteen-year-old. "I can see him."

"Are his grays hitched to the curricle?" whispered Miss Honoria Weyland, a fair-haired seventeen-year-old with pale skin prone to freckles. She fixed her bright eyes on her informer with avid interest.

Lady Jane Hatchard, a long-faced child with dark

hair and a supercilious gaze, wrinkled her nose. "Only you'd care about such a paltry thing as that."

"Paltry! Why, I daresay they are almost as famous as he is," asserted the indignant Miss Weyland.

"How has he tied his neckcloth?" demanded the plump and quite pretty Miss Hanna Brookstone in hushed tones that carried all too well. Several giggles answered this question.

"Silly. I can't see it from here," said Miss Middleton. "He's wearing a driving coat, though, and it has upwards of sixteen capes, and the largest, shiniest buttons I have ever seen."

"No, has it, really?" Miss Brookstone sprang to her feet. "Is he wearing his Hessians? And are they shining so one can see one's face in them?"

Phoebe stood, straightening to her full, if decidedly uncommanding, height. "You will oblige me," she said in icy tones, "by coming away from the window and not behaving as if you were raised in a stable yard."

"That is only Honoria," declared Lady Jane.

"But it is Rushmere!" cried Miss Middleton, making no move to obey her preceptress's injunction. "He has come to take Juliana on a visit to her grandmother, for the old lady hasn't been well. It's been in the papers, you know, that the dowager marchioness has been staying here in Bath to take the waters, and that Rushmere has been in frequent attendance upon her."

"In Laura Place," added the well-informed Miss Brookstone.

Phoebe regarded them with disapproval. "Your behavior goes beyond polite interest. You seem to think a marquis is a raree at a fair."

"Not just *any* marquis," explained Miss Middleton in the tone of a social superior explaining the obvious to a hopeless outsider. "It is Rushmere. Even you must be aware he is a noted Corinthian."

"A Nonpareil," added Miss Weyland in a voice of awe.

"A widower," stuck in the socially aware Miss Brookstone. "It is a pity he is so very old. He must be five-and-thirty if he is a day."

Miss Sophronia Farnham sighed. "What does that matter? He is quite the handsomest gentleman I have ever seen."

"You think *every* gentleman you see is the handsomest," came Lady Jane's prompt and withering response.

"Well, Rushmere is—is—" Miss Farnham faltered, searching her limited vocabulary for words to express her opinion.

The embodiment of the dream of every schoolroom miss, reflected Phoebe. Not to mention every schoolroom instructress. She'd indulged in a few daydreams herself, since first she'd encountered him in the office of the Misses Crippenham. He'd seemed the ideal—

A horrid realization thrust itself into her mind. The Marquis of Rushmere had been eclipsed, his perfect Corinthian image fading before that of another, less noble but more commanding, gentleman. The devil take Sir Miles Saunderton, she fumed. How dare he invade her private daydreams. And how dare the mere thought of him set her pulse beating faster.

It had to be with anger, she reassured herself. He was far too disagreeable to stir any other emotion within her. What she really needed was to encounter Rushmere again, to allow his obvious good breeding and elegant appearance to soothe her ruffled composure. Of course, the only time she'd been introduced to him, when he'd been awaiting his thirteen-year-old daughter on a previous occasion, he had barely acknowledged her. But that was only to be expected in a nobleman of his rank.

"He's the handsomest!" finished Miss Farhnam, giving up the struggle.

"And he is a leader of society," added Miss Middleton, "which you would know, Miss Caldicot, had you ever been to London. Even if he weren't a marquis, he'd still be important."

"And handsome," asserted Miss Farhnam.

"He is a hardened rake!" pronounced the whey-faced Miss Amabel Grisham in tones of disdain. "I have not the least interest in seeing him."

"That's because you're such a baby. You're only fourteen," laughed Lady Jane, from the lofty advantage of being almost eighteen months her senior. "Besides, what would you know of him? Or of rakes, for that matter?"

"And what makes you think it is acceptable to speak of such things?" demanded Phoebe, without much hope of being attended to.

"I do know," persisted Miss Grisham. "Better than any of you. He danced with my sister Louisa once, and she said he flirted with her in the most outrageous manner, and put her to the blush so many times she was near to tears."

"Louisa Grisham is always near to tears," exclaimed

Miss Middleton. "She's a pea goose. My brother says so."

"Your brother—" began Lady Jane, but the girl subsided under the quelling glare directed at her by Phoebe.

"That is quite enough of that." Phoebe strode to the window and pulled the curtains. A useless gesture, she knew, for the marquis had long since disappeared within doors, denying her the chance of a glimpse of him, as well. But he would come out again, and as much as she might be tempted to imitate Miss Middleton and peek out the window at this elegant personage, she would do no such thing. Nor, she determined as she turned back to the room, would she permit her charges to so indulge themselves, either. "Now, I presume, since you all have so much time to fritter away on gossip, that you have each completed your letters? If so, then you will not mind writing an invitation to a house party, which I expect you to hand to me before you meet with Mademoiselle Dupre for your French lessons."

A series of groans greeted this pronouncement, but Phoebe had the satisfaction of seeing the young ladies return to their tasks with determination, if not with enthusiasm. That would do, Phoebe reflected.

The marquis would be gone by the time she went downstairs to the music room, where she next must spend a painful hour or more instructing her young ladies upon the pianoforte. A pity, for a glimpse of him would have quite brightened her day. Repressing a sigh, she returned to her desk and resumed her interrupted task of trying to decipher the illegible scrawls of Miss Honoria Weyland.

She had not been at this long when Mademoiselle Dupre herself came in, saying she was to sit with the girls while Phoebe attended the Misses Crippenham in their office. A stab of panic pierced Phoebe's usual calm, but she managed to quell it. She would be reprimanded, of course; she expected it. But it wouldn't be more than that. The ladies probably wished to discuss Lucilla's withdrawal from the Academy. It was even likely they would inform her she would have a new pupil arriving to begin classes on the morrow. Their academy enjoyed an exalted reputation—probably because of their rigid discipline and high standards.

She made her way down the stairs and noted with a touch of regret that the marquis was nowhere in sight. Well, she must count what blessings she possessed. At least there wasn't any Miles Saunderton lingering about to make her morning any more unpleasant. She knocked on the office door, then entered in response to the call from within.

Both the Misses Crippenham sat behind the great desk, upon which only a very few papers lay in a neat stack. The surface was so tidy, it always made Phoebe uncomfortable. Everything about the room screamed precision: books lined up in perfect rows on the shelves, chairs stood at identical angles, the triple-branched candelabrum rested in the exact center of the occasional table, which in turn stood exactly midway along the side wall.

The two ladies, when seen together, bore a striking

resemblance to one another. Though Miss Crippenham, on the verge of her sixtieth birthday, possessed features less sharp than her younger sister's, their eyes shared an uncompromising, steady stare. Daughters of dukes had been known to quail beneath their regard. They might wear their graying hair in different styles, Miss Aurelia's in a braided crown and Miss Crippenham's in a chignon, but the same precise neatness characterized both. In matters of dress, though, Miss Crippenham proved herself the less austere; her dove gray gown boasted a knot of ribands and—daringly—a narrow flounce.

At the moment, neither of the two ladies radiated good will. Miss Aurelia, the younger by three years, regarded Phoebe without speaking, her expression stern. Her elder sister emitted a sigh eloquent of resigned disappointment. "We have had Sir Miles Saunderton with us this morning," she said.

Phoebe's heart sank. Yet even these high sticklers for the proprieties could hardly blame her for Lucilla's escapade. But in that, she found herself wrong.

Miss Crippenham cleared her throat. "You have been shockingly remiss in your duties, Miss Caldicot," she said with a note of sincere regret. "That is something we do not tolerate at our academy."

"Not in anyone," added Miss Aurelia. "Lucilla Saunderton has been sent away."

"But I thought her brother had come to remove her—" Phoebe began.

"Sent away," asserted Miss Aurelia. "Her brother has decided to launch her into society in an attempt to avert any gossip concerning her dismissal from our academy."

Phoebe kept her mouth shut. Sir Miles had arrived the previous evening with the intention already formed to take his sister to London immediately. Yet the last thing she wanted at the moment was to antagonize her employers. *After* Thomas graduated, she promised herself. After he had secured a living.

"We cannot allow a repetition of the shocking occurrences of last night," contributed Miss Crippenham. "It would never do if parents felt they could not trust the safety of their daughters to the vigilance of our staff."

"It would never do at all," agreed her sister. "Therefore," and she said this with considerable relish, "it is obvious there is only one course open to us. Your employment, Miss Caldicot, is terminated, as of this moment."

Two

Her employment terminated. The words echoed through Phoebe's mind, heard over and over, yet making absolutely no sense at all. They *couldn't* make any sense. She simply could not have lost her job. She needed it too desperately.

Miss Aurelia, her expression that of one who had satisfied her outrage, held out several coins. "Your pay, through today. Good day to you, Miss Caldicot. And goodbye."

"We trust you will have vacated your room by this evening," added Miss Crippenham. "Such a bother to be obliged to search for a new instructress, but I make no doubt we shall find one quickly."

Quickly. To be replaced so easily. Shock rendered Phoebe immobile, followed at once by outraged indignation.

Miss Aurelia lowered her hand, the coins still in it, and frowned at her. "If you wish to say something, Miss Caldicot, kindly speak up and stop gaping at us as if you were a stuffed trout."

"Most unpleasant," agreed Miss Crippenham with a reproachful frown.

Nothing she said or did would make any difference, Phoebe realized. No difference whatsoever. She stared for a moment longer at the cold, closed face of Miss Aurelia, at the regretful yet equally unyielding expression of Miss Crippenham, then turned on her heel and stalked from the room.

She mounted the stairs with dragging feet, still stunned. She'd never actually been happy here, but she'd thought she had some measure of security. She'd had her pay—

Her pay. She hadn't taken her pay, and she needed every penny coming to her. Later, she decided; she would collect it when she left this place and shook its dust from her proverbial sandals. She wasn't about to go back down to them at this moment.

She found she had reached her room and stepped inside, looking about the cozy apartment she'd created from the bare, functional room she'd been given. Home, she'd thought each time she'd come through that door. But not anymore.

She sank onto the bed, staring about her. She had to pack, to leave—

Anger at the unfairness of her treatment didn't counterbalance the pain at leaving this sanctuary she had carved for herself. She reached out, touching the padded arm of her favorite chair. How could she take her furniture, when she had no idea of where she could go? Perhaps Thomas—

Thomas. She closed her eyes. Dear God, Thomas. How would she tell her brother? How would she be able to help him pay his school fees for another term? And longer than that. Two more years stretched before them, before he could be ordained and begin earning the pittance allotted to a minor curate. He must finish his schooling. Which meant that somehow, she must find the means to help him pay for it.

But how did one do that when dismissed from one's post, and most likely without a character?

She shivered, chilled, more from reaction and distress, she realized, than from the actual temperature of the room, though that wasn't as warm as she could wish. The urge hit her to light a fire, in defiance of the rules that forbade such a luxury during the day, but not so much as a single faggot lay beside her hearth.

Yet the idea of fire, of light, called to her. Numbly, she leaned across to the blue-and-white porcelain chamberstick she had possessed since she was a child, groped for her tinderbox, and struck a flame. It hovered, then caught, and a warm, golden glow haloed about it, flickering then steadying as the wax burned cleanly up the wick. She gazed into the light, as she had on so many other occasions, and an all-enveloping tiredness seeped through her.

One positive side existed to all this, she assured herself with an attempt at her usual humor. At least she would not have to bear with another haughty, spoiled young lady on the brink of making her curtsy to the *haut ton*. The girls failed to see why they should listen to a preceptress who had no practical experience of the social maze they were about to tread, and some of them felt no compunction whatsoever about telling her so. She would not miss them in the least.

She would miss the security, though. If she had a

wish, just one wish that could be miraculously granted, it would be to escape this life of uncertainty, to know her brother's future safe. And for herself? The longing for a real home of her own filled her, for a family and—dare she dream so much?—for love. But these were all denied to a young lady of no fortune and no opportunities.

The flame flickered, then steadied; her thoughts shifted from the impossible but wonderful to the probable but bleak. Dreams of marriage were naught but a waste of time. She would register with an employment agency that afternoon, begin the soul-scarring task of seeking a new position at once. Yet she already knew, all too well, that no employment available to an impoverished lady of quality would pay a sufficient wage for her to help Thomas.

Which brought her back to marriage as her only other option. Yet she knew no eligible gentlemen, only the fathers and brothers of her pupils, the former already married, the latter generally too young—or in one case she could think of, too disagreeable—to take an interest in one of their sisters' instructresses.

Of course, there was the Marquis of Rushmere. That thought almost made her smile. True, he was a widower, but despite what one learned in tales of fairy godmothers, handsome, wealthy noblemen did *not* marry penniless, unemployed schoolmistresses. If only there were such a thing as a fairy godmother. On that whimsical thought, she extinguished her candle and headed for the lumber room where she had stowed her solitary trunk upon taking up her residence at the Misses Crippenham's Academy.

The retrieval of this object ultimately required the assistance of Henry, the elderly footman employed by the parsimonious Misses Crippenham to lend a note of formality to their establishment. He asked no questions, for which Phoebe was grateful, but she feared it was because he was already in full possession of the facts. Together they dragged her case along the hall to her room, setting it to rest at last on the throw rug in the center of the floor.

Phoebe eyed it without enthusiasm. Then, with a sigh, she set to work placing her books in the bottom. Where she would take them out again, she had no idea. For that matter, she did not even know where to spend this night.

This serious problem still occupied her mind, with little positive result, when a light tap sounded on her door. It opened at once to admit Annie, the maid of all work who waited upon the instructresses. Her wide eyes glittered with curiosity as she cast a rapid glance about the chaos of Phoebe's room.

"If you please, miss," said Annie, "there's a lady, Lady Xanthe Simms, arrived to speak to you. I asked her to wait in the salon, but I don't like to think what will happen if either Miss Crippenham or Miss Aurelia should walk in on her. Ever so snippy as they are this morning."

"Lady Xanthe Simms?" murmured Phoebe, dragged from her depressing reflections. "Are you quite certain it was me she wanted to see, Annie?"

"Yes, miss. And such a lady."

Phoebe rose from where she knelt beside the chest and made a valiant attempt to brush the wrinkles from her dress and the smudges from her hands. "Thank you, Annie," she said, and hurried from the room, all the while wracking her memory for a clue to her visitor's identity.

But try as she might, she could not remember ever hearing the lady's name before. She had no idea . . . unless she might have something to do with Lucilla Saunderton's officer from last night. Her spirits, which had already been riding at low ebb, sank even farther toward the soles of her shoes. She reached the entry hall, cast a quick glance in the gilt-trimmed mirror, which hung above an occasional table, to assure herself her long hair remained neatly in its chignon, then turned to the salon and this mysterious visitor.

She opened the door, only to pause on the threshold, frowning slightly as she studied the amused countenance of the woman waiting within. The face remained wholly unfamiliar. Phoebe's gaze darted quickly over her, noting the profuse amounts of roped hair more golden than yellow, the elegant carriage of the head, and a traveling gown of bottle green merino, so simply cut and perfectly fitted that it could only have come from the hands of a *modiste* of the first stare. She tried to fathom what such a personage could want with her, and failed utterly.

As she took a step into the room, she realized that the penetrating regard of a pair of very fine violet eyes rested on her, taking in each detail in a manner every bit as comprehensive as her own had been. Warmth flushed her cheeks, but she kept her head high. "Lady Xanthe?" she asked, the calmness of her voice belying the sudden, inexplicable flutter of nerves in her stomach. "How may I be of service to you?"

An irresistible dimple peeped at the corner of the woman's mouth. "On the contrary, my dear. I have come to be of service to you." She rose from her chair with ineffable grace and seemed to float toward Phoebe, her hands extended. "I am your godmother, my dear child. Your *fairy* godmother, to be exact. I have come in answer to your wish."

"My—" Phoebe blinked, taken aback. "Indeed," she managed after a moment. "My *fairy* godmother. To be sure. Of course you are." She accepted the pressure of the hands that clasped hers, and found it oddly reassuring.

The violet eyes twinkled with barely suppressed merriment. "You don't believe me," the little woman said. "Well, I'm not surprised. The situation is a trifle unusual, I suppose."

Phoebe watched her, not sure whether to be fascinated by, or afraid of, her unconventional visitor. "A trifle," she agreed. "What, precisely, is the difference between a fairy godmother and a regular one?"

Lady Xanthe laughed, an intriguing, musical sound. "My dearest child, I can do so much more than a mere ordinary godmother. I know the dearest wish of your heart."

Phoebe raised her eyebrows in polite disbelief. "Indeed? I suppose you believe I wish for love."

"Love is its own magic." Xanthe shook her head. "All I can offer is the opportunity. But your wish, as you must remember perfectly well, was for a chance to provide an education for your brother and security for yourself."

Phoebe, who had started to sit on a chair, straightened in surprise. "How did you know?"

"You made your wish over a candle in your room." Lady Xanthe resumed her seat, but her amused gaze lingered on Phoebe. "I have come to grant you the opportunity to make your wish come true."

"But—" Phoebe broke off, shaking her head, and seated herself. The situation was preposterous. The wish of someone in her position must be obvious to anyone, and gazing into a candle flame would be a very likely time to daydream about desires. She'd done it often. Any number of explanations existed for how her visitor had guessed so correctly. For a guess it had to be.

Lady Xanthe shook her head. "Belief is difficult, is it not, my dear? Never mind, it will come. The important thing for now is that you make a precise wish— how, exactly, you want to achieve your security. And you did, you know," she added with a touch of mischief, "think wistfully of marriage and a family."

Warm color suffused Phoebe's cheeks. "And if I made this specific wish for a husband?"

"You may wish for a *chance* to find one," came the smiling answer.

"A chance," Phoebe breathed. That was more than she'd ever had before. "Then, I would not have to name someone specific?" she ventured.

Xanthe laughed, a soft, warming sound. "Of course not, my dear. You know so very few gentlemen, situated as you are."

"And how am I ever to have a chance to meet some-one?"

Lady Xanthe's eyes twinkled in the light that filtered into the room. "Why, how does any young lady of quality meet a potential husband?"

"In London, I suppose. During the Season."

"Then, that is where you shall go."

Phoebe blinked. "But it is quite beyond my means."

"Not if your godmother invites you to spend the Season in town with her," came Xanthe's prompt response.

"But I do not have a—" She broke off, her eyes widening.

Xanthe beamed at her. "Precisely, my love. I have come to take you to town for the Season."

Phoebe straightened in her chair. "I beg your pardon?"

"London," Lady Xanthe repeated helpfully. "The Season. You shall be my guest."

"But—" Phoebe stared at her, coherent thought alien to the chaos in her mind. "London," she repeated, her voice hollow. *"Why?"*

"Because, as you said, that is where you shall have the greatest chance to make your wish come true. Because you would dearly love such a visit for its own sake. And because I love granting opportunities. It is what I do."

"To—to be sure," Phoebe said weakly. She stared at her visitor, this remarkable little woman who had burst into her world which had so recently fallen apart, offering her an escape, a haven for at least the next two months, the opportunity for which she secretly had longed. It was too good to be true.

A *fairy* godmother?

"What is the price?" she asked abruptly.

"Price?" Lady Xanthe's brow creased. "Oh, you mean the conditions. There aren't any, really. Only something you must understand. You see, magic alone is not enough."

"I see." Disappointment, unexpected but very real, seeped through her. It *had* been too good to be true.

Lady Xanthe fixed her with a very serious look. "As I told you, magic can only provide opportunities, my dear. The use you make of those opportunities is entirely up to you."

"I see." Phoebe considered. "So you don't *really* grant wishes at all."

Xanthe shook her head, smiling. "Dear child," she said softly, "no one has the power to do that but you yourself. And you do have that power. What you lack—or at least what you lacked until now—is the opportunity. That is what I am able to grant you."

"But what if I am not able to find a husband? I have neither fortune nor lofty connections to recommend me."

"There is nothing amiss with your family," Lady Xanthe pointed out.

"But it is not important enough to overcome my want of fortune. Or rather, my debt, for I must help my brother finish at Cambridge."

Lady Xanthe regarded her solemnly. "If you cannot find a husband, my dear, then you will find yourself as you are now, except you will always know that you wasted your opportunity."

Not very secure, this chance of hers for security. Yet it was the best offer she was likely to receive. She met Xanthe's serious gaze. "I will do my best."

"Then, we shall make a covenant." Xanthe held out her hands, and a flickering flame sprang to life between them.

Phoebe gasped. "How—?" Then she added under her breath, in a voice of bemused comprehension, "A *fairy* godmother."

"You will become accustomed to the idea, my dearest child. Take the flame."

Phoebe reached out hesitant hands, and the fire seemed to fly through the intervening air to settle between her fingers. No heat burned her, but her palms tingled. Through it, haloed by the light, she could see Lady Xanthe's smiling face.

"Do you swear to make the most of the opportunity I offer? Do you undertake to accept an offer of marriage before the end of the Season?"

Without giving herself time for further reflection, Phoebe took the plunge. "I swear," she breathed.

The ball of flame exploded in a soundless burst of glittering light. Phoebe watched the myriad particles settle toward the carpet, but they vanished before reaching it. Uncertainly she reached down, but her questing fingers encountered nothing.

"There, it is settled," Lady Xanthe told her. "You will accompany me to London for the Season."

"London," Phoebe breathed. For a moment, her thoughts drifted from the magical flame she had just seen, flying to balls and ridottos, *al fresco* breakfasts and musical *soirees,* all the events about which her pupils dreamed, but in which she'd always known she could never take part. And, like every other young lady, she hoped to meet someone she could esteem, perhaps even love. . . . The prospect both thrilled and frightened her. Somewhere, in London, lay a secure and happy future for her—and for Thomas, as well. She only had to find and claim it.

So easy to say, so difficult to do. . . .

She squared her shoulders. "When do we leave?"

"At once. We shall spend tonight at the York Hotel, then the next on the road, and arrive in Half Moon Street by the following evening."

"I must still finish my packing," Phoebe warned.

A reprehensible dimple appeared in Lady Xanthe's left cheek. "I am afraid I have taken the liberty of finishing it for you. You will find your trunk corded and already strapped to the back of my carriage."

Phoebe blinked. "Being a *fairy* godmother would seem to have a few advantages."

"Yes." The mischievous smile flashed. "I have always thought so. It can make everything so very simple."

Simple. Magic was simple? Leaping from complete disaster to the chance of her lifetime was simple? Finding someone to marry—to love—was simple?

Excitement bubbled within her, which required a serious effort to keep in check. It didn't seem possible. It *couldn't* be possible. Only an hour or so ago she'd been regretting that fairy godmothers didn't really exist. And now here, before her, sat a very real one, answering her wish. She became aware of a soft humming and realized the sweet melody came from Xanthe.

The woman smiled at her, continued for a moment longer, then abruptly broke off and rose. "We might as well be off. Would you care for a quarter of an hour or so to say goodbye to those with whom you have grown close?" The dimple peeped out again. "And one or two of your pupils might be interested to know where you are bound. Oh, and do you care for your pearls?"

"My—" Phoebe's hand groped at her throat and encountered a cool strand of smooth, round beads that had not been there a moment before. With fumbling fingers she found the catch and held the creamy necklace before her, staring at it in disbelief.

"They will vanish when your wish is complete, I fear. But you may enjoy them until then. And now, run and make your farewells. I will await you in the carriage."

Hastily, Phoebe came to her feet as well, still clutching the pearls. Words, all inadequate to the occasion, raced through her mind, utterly failing to find voice. Lady Xanthe leaned forward and planted a whispery kiss on her cheek. Then she stood back, humming softly, a different tune this time, as an iridescent glow surrounded her. It grew until it extended a good three feet from her, then burst in a cascade of shimmering particles that evaporated before they hit the floor.

Lady Xanthe had vanished.

But the soft humming lingered for several moments longer, wrapping about Phoebe like an inexplicable joy. And something else remained, something that glinted on the carpet where Xanthe had staged her impressive exit, something shiny that caught and glittered in a ray of sunlight that filtered through the window. Phoebe stooped and picked up a round feather, about two inches in diameter, almost transparent except for a slight iridescence and a golden tip. She turned it between her fingers.

A fairy godmother. Lady Xanthe really was a fairy godmother. And she would grant Phoebe's dearest wish. Tomorrow she would really set forth for London, really experience the wonders of the social season, and—perhaps—receive the offer of marriage that would assure both her security and her happiness. With a mischievous smile of her own, she set off to bid a fond goodbye to Annie and Henry, and to inform Miss Georgeana Middleton—and perhaps Lady Jane, as well—of her destination.

After a night of surprisingly restful sleep at the York Hotel, they set forth at a comfortably advanced hour of the morning. To Phoebe's delight, traveling with a fairy godmother proved unlike anything she had experienced before. For one thing, the drive never had a chance to become tedious. Xanthe would begin to hum, and suddenly the grass on the verge might turn a bright scarlet, or the cows in a pasture might sport chip straw bonnets, or the branches of a tree might fill with marigolds or fans, or whatever whimsy took the mischievous fairy's fancy. Once a flock of blackbirds on the wing diverted their route to perform an amazing display of aerial acrobatics just beside their carriage. Another time, a pair of doves, their feathers gleaming white, landed on the open window and appeared to carry on a conversation with Xanthe.

And then there was Titus. The huge white cat spent most of the journey curled on a deep purple cushion placed just for his use on the facing seat. Xanthe addressed frequent comments to him, to which the cat uttered a series of sounds, or merely twitched the end of his tail. That they understood one another perfectly, Phoebe had not a single doubt. She watched their interchanges in fascination, and deemed herself favored when, after a stop to change horses, the giant feline deigned to spread his considerable bulk in her lap.

Xanthe watched with smiling approval. "He likes you," she said.

"I'm honored." And Phoebe found she actually meant it.

Titus looked up at her, the cool blue of his eyes assessing, considering. He blinked in slow motion, yawned, and went to sleep.

Their nuncheon proved an event to remember. No stopping at coaching inns for Xanthe. As soon as Phoebe began to grow hungry, her godmother ordered the carriage to pull off the road at a place where a meadow, with an imposing old oak, stretched off to one side. Xanthe hummed a lively tune, and a table, laid with linen, china and silver, appeared beneath the tree.

Liveried footmen in powdered wigs opened the door and handed them to their places. Others presented them with delicate wines and a series of covered dishes that revealed new potatoes in a cream and herb sauce, minted peas, and slivers of something that might have been a savory roast duckling, except that Xanthe shunned the eating of what she termed her "fellow creatures." Fresh raspberries—still out of season, but for Xanthe perfectly ripe—and chilled champagne made up the final course, and Phoebe returned to the carriage feeling as content and sleepy as Titus.

"You are spoiling me," she told Xanthe as they settled once more on the velvet cushions of the well-sprung traveling coach.

Her fairy godmother beamed at her. "I always feel one should be allowed to enjoy magic when one has the chance. It comes into most people's lives so seldom."

And Phoebe could only be grateful it had come into hers at all.

They broke their journey at an amazingly comfortable inn, and rose at an hour that Phoebe, inured to the hardships of an instructress, considered sinfully decadent. Fresh rolls hot from the oven, honey, sliced fruit and tea comprised their breakfast. As they emerged out-of-doors at last to resume their journey, lowering clouds met them, and a chill drizzle threatened to make travel unpleasant. The innkeeper himself placed hot bricks at their feet—bricks, Phoebe realized about an hour later, that remained toasty hot.

The drizzle all too soon turned to rain. At least, it turned to rain everywhere except in the immediate vicinity of the moving carriage. There the drops turned to flowers, tiny snowdrops, bluebells, daisies, and a score of other blossoms Phoebe couldn't quite make out. She turned to peer out the window behind them, only to see nothing but the muddy road.

The weather—and the flowers—finally cleared, and a flock of pigeons took their place, accompanying them for a number of miles, roosting on the carriage or flying intricate patterns in turn. At about one o'clock they partook of another *al fresco* nuncheon, every bit as sumptuous as the day's before, then resumed their journey, the monotony broken frequently by Xanthe-inspired absurdities in the landscape. At last, as the early darkness closed about them, they reached the outskirts of London. Phoebe sat forward, peering at the unfamiliar buildings, the people that seemed to fill the streets. She couldn't help but wonder if any of this would ever feel real.

"We shall go shopping in the morning," Xanthe said at last, breaking a long silence. "I have been considering the *modistes,* and have decided that Madame Bernadette will be the most suitable to turn you out in the first style of elegance."

Phoebe turned from the carriage window. "You will not simply conjure me a wardrobe?"

"I could." Xanthe tilted her head to one side, laughter in her eyes. "But such gowns would only last for the duration of our stay in London. And since I know you have long wished to experience the sort of Season your pupils will face, we cannot possibly omit anything so fundamental as visiting the fashionable *modistes* and milliners."

Somehow, that had more the sound of a threat than a rare treat, but Phoebe refrained from comment. Her attention refocused on the innumerable carriages and wagons which filled the streets through which they maneuvered, the shop windows with their displays of luggage, of silver, of books, of boots and clothing. Then they turned onto a quieter road lined with elegant town houses, and the bustle and noise receded.

After several more turns the carriage slowed, then pulled to a stop. Even as the groom swung from his position beside the coachman, the door of one of the houses swung wide, and a majordomo, flanked by two footmen wearing the same livery as the magical servants who had waited on them for their *al fresco* nuncheons, hurried down the stairs. One footman opened the carriage door for them, while the other aided the groom in unstrapping Phoebe's trunk.

Phoebe herself stepped down to the cobbled stones, looking about her with avid interest. The notes of a haunting melody seeped into her mind, and she cast a quick glance at Xanthe, wondering what her godmother was about. But the woman conversed with the majordomo, not humming at all.

The footmen started up the stairs with their burden; and as Xanthe followed them inside, the door to the neighboring house opened, and a gentleman, resplendent in plain black evening dress, a black cloak, and an elegant cane in his gloved hands, emerged onto the porch. He cast a casual glance in her direction, then stopped, staring at Phoebe. After a moment, he descended the steps and strolled toward her. He had almost reached her before she recognized Sir Miles Saunderton.

Of all people— Shock hit her; she could think of no one she would less like to encounter again. Then anger washed over her, for what had passed between them at their last meeting, for what he must have said to the Misses Crippenham, for the undeniable fact that if it had not been for him catching her trying to break into the Academy, she would still be gainfully employed and able to help support her brother.

Sir Miles halted before her and swept her an elegant bow. "I had not expected the pleasure of seeing you again so soon, Miss Caldicot."

"Pleasure?" She glared at him. "I would hardly call it that."

His eyebrows rose quizzically. "But common politeness demands that we say such things."

"Common politeness can—" She broke off, glaring at him. No gentleman so disagreeable had any right to have such compelling eyes, such ruggedly handsome features.

A muscle at the corner of his mouth twitched. "I beg your pardon. But what brings you to town? I had thought you still in Bath."

The mildness of his tone, the complete lack of constraint in his manner, proved too much for her. The trauma, the emotions of the last few days, and the uncertainties, fears, and excitement welled within her, demanding an outlet. Her temper exploded, catching him in its shrapnel.

"How dare you?" she demanded. "How dare you stand there mouthing inanities as if it were not all your fault?"

"My fault?" His brow snapped down. "May I ask what it is you think you are talking about?"

"I lost my job because of you! Yes, at least you

have the decency to stare at that. It may not seem important to you, but it is to me. Excessively so. And all I had to console myself with was the certain knowledge I would never have to lay eyes upon you again! And now here you are, where you are least wanted, the very first person I encounter upon my arrival in London."

He had been watching her, his expression changing from surprised to intrigued. "That does seem rather unfair," he said with a gravity that caused him a noticeable effort.

"Unfair? *Unfair?* It is monstrous! Please tell me you were only visiting in that house next door to my godmother's!" she implored.

"I regret to be forced to disoblige you, Miss Caldicot. That is something I cannot do."

"You—you *live* there?"

He inclined his head, his smile becoming more pronounced. "I fear I do."

A vexed exclamation escaped her. Her hands clenched, and for a long moment she glared at him. Then she turned on her heel and stormed into the house. From behind her, she could hear a deep, rumbling chuckle.

And what was worse, he still had the most heart-melting smile she had ever encountered.

Three

A laugh of sheer joy welled in Phoebe as she drew in a deep, aching breath of the chill morning air. Freedom. A chance to work out the lingering anger from the evening before. A chance to rediscover some measure of peace, which she had not experienced for so very long. Here, she might be riding across the countryside, riding to the wind, rather than following the circuit of Hyde Park. And it was vastly satisfying to know she had been correct in what she had told her pupils, that few people really did come here at the unconscionable hour of seven in the morning so early in the Season. So far, she had passed three grooms exercising their employers' cattle. No one else. Not one other single solitary soul. After five years in the cramped quarters of the Misses Crippenham's Academy, her country-bred soul relished the solitude.

And at the moment, solitude was just as well. She'd come to try out the paces of the mare provided for her by Lady Xanthe, and a rare handful the animal proved to be. No dainty lady's mount, this; Xanthe, as always, knew what suited her best. Phoebe had been practically raised in a saddle. The horse stood nearly seventeen hands at the wither, with a fine, sloping shoulder and powerful hindquarters. Her coat gleamed a satiny black. A devil mount, had warned Limmer, Lady Xanthe's groom, but Phoebe disagreed. Macha, Xanthe had named the mare, after an Irish goddess of war, and that suited her to perfection. Not vile-tempered in the least, but strong-hearted and high-spirited.

Phoebe touched lightly on the reins, catching the arrogant head that tossed to have its own way. They would come to an understanding soon enough, she knew. At the moment, though, after so many years of riding nothing but the staid, suitable mounts at the Academy, she delighted in the subtle shifting of power between herself and the willful mare. Nothing, she reflected, could ruin this morning.

The head dropped—straight down—and the back arched as the animal bounded in a series of crow hops. Playful, Phoebe noted as she spurred the mare forward to put an end to these tricks. No intention to harm, but more to test and challenge and let off excess energy. They both fretted for exercise.

Phoebe spared her attention from her fractious mount and glanced about. She could see no one except the stoic Limmer, who rode several lengths behind, his calculating eye watching them with grudging respect. "I'm going to give her her head," Phoebe called over her shoulder.

The wiry little man frowned, an occupation that seemed to involve his entire weathered countenance. He, too, cast a rapid glance about, then pursed his thin lips. "Just a short ways, miss. You don't want her to go thinking she can make a race of it every time she comes here. Wouldn't do at all."

"Only when we're alone," Phoebe promised, and eased her hold.

At once, the black muzzle thrust forward, and through her touch on the reins Phoebe felt Macha grasp the bit between her teeth. The strides lengthened with fluid grace, and a thrill of pure joy rushed through Phoebe as the powerful muscles bunched beneath her. She leaned low, welcoming the air that whipped past, tangling the tendrils of hair that escaped from the modish riding hat provided by Xanthe that morning. Behind her, she could hear the pounding hooves of Limmer's mount, falling back, unable to keep pace.

Then another horseman, springing toward her from where the trees had half hidden him, joined the race. Admiration filled her for this gentleman's mount, a red roan of passionate enthusiasm, determined not to be outdone. The rider veered to intercept her. For a few breathless moments they raced neck to neck; then the roan pulled ahead as its rider flung himself forward to grasp Phoebe's rein.

Abruptly the roan broke pace, slowed to a trot, then came to a halt. Macha spun about, throwing her head in protest, jerking free of the man's restraining hand. For a very long minute Phoebe had her hands full bringing the rebellious mare back under control.

When at last her mount stood trembling beneath her, she glared at her accoster, and recognition did nothing to soothe her rising temper. "You!" she breathed in pure loathing.

"Good God," said Sir Miles, and he looked rather taken aback. A lopsided smile lit his face.

That irritatingly attractive half smile of his. What business did a man like this have with a smile that could plant her a leveler, in the boxing cant favored by her pupils' brothers? Her indignation fueled her anger, and she exclaimed, "How dare you catch my rein!"

Sir Miles's eyebrows flew upward, and a pair of brilliant hazel eyes glinted golden in sudden amusement. "I thought I had just performed a rescue," he said. His deep voice held a note of something that might have been either humor or irritation, or possibly both.

"Rescue!" Phoebe sniffed. "I haven't needed rescuing since I was four! You have quite ruined my gallop, and as for my mare—!"

The gentleman sat back in his saddle, his amusement growing. "It is not considered proper to gallop in the park," he pointed out on a note of apology. "I should have thought that was one of the points on which you had to instruct your pupils."

Her chin rose. "Indeed it is—or rather was, thanks to your interference. And it seems I know the rules more perfectly than do you. During the hour of the Promenade I should never dream to do so, of course. Or at a time when it is more populous than now. But it is quite permissible to exercise one's horses at so early an hour as this. *And,*" she added pointedly, "without interference."

"Sa, sa," he murmured the fencer's acknowledgment, his eyes gleaming. Then aloud, he added, "I beg your pardon."

Phoebe eyed him with the resentment of one who suspects she is being laughed at. "And so you should. Do you make a habit of accosting anyone who indulges in a gallop?"

The golden lights in his eyes danced. "I make it a habit of helping when someone appears to be in need of aid. It seems I misjudged the situation, and must apologize."

Phoebe frowned, vexation replacing her anger. "Did I indeed seem out of control?"

The gentleman hesitated. "Perhaps," he said after a moment, "had there been the leisure to observe your handling of your mount, I might have realized the truth. As it was, I noted only the break-neck pace and the absence of any attendant. I sprang to the wrong conclusion."

"Absence of—" Phoebe began, only to break off. Then, "Oh, the devil!" she exclaimed, reverting to the language culled during her illicit childhood forays into the hunting field. She craned about in her saddle, and Macha shifted beneath her. "Where has poor Limmer gotten— Ah!" Even as she spoke, she glimpsed his chestnut trotting toward them. "Poor man, but he hadn't a hope of keeping up."

"Then, why did you career off like that? It may, indeed, be permissible to gallop at such an hour, but I assure you, it is *not* permissible for a young lady to ride in the park without some form of chaperonage."

Phoebe, who had begun to unruffle her feathers, stiffened once more. "Indeed?" she said, her tone frigid. "Do you often inform other people how they ought to behave?"

That finally pierced his good humor. He regarded her from beneath a furrowed brow, as if the possibility revolted him. "I do no such thing!"

Phoebe bowed her head in mock contrition. "I see. I quite mistook your words. I do so humbly beg your pardon."

He regarded her in patent exasperation. "Just because I venture to comment upon—"

"Comment?" she interrupted. "You as much as told me I behaved improperly!"

"Well, had you been here without a groom, you would have done," he pointed out with an air of infuriating reasonableness.

"But here is my groom, as you may see for yourself." She regarded Sir Miles in triumph at having carried her point.

"Now, yes," he agreed. "But he was very much not in evidence when you dashed heedless along the tanbark, which is what made it seem so very probable your horse had run away with you."

She eyed him sternly, and asked with a sweetness resembling treacle, "I suppose you expect me to thank you?"

At that, a deep, rich, contagious laugh escaped him. "Miss Caldicot, I am not so mad as to expect any such thing."

She inclined her head with cold austerity. "I am quite relieved to hear it."

"That is a prime bit of horseflesh." He regarded her mount with a considering eye. "Restive, though," he added as the mare sidled, tossing her head to be away. "I quite see why you indulged her in a gallop."

"I am so relieved," she said with heavy sarcasm, then stroked the gleaming neck. "She hates to be still," she added pointedly. "One can understand how she feels."

"Perhaps we should walk them," he suggested. This time, his gaze rested on Phoebe's face.

"An excellent notion, though I doubt she would be content with just that. Good morning, sir." She gave him a dismissive nod, turned the mare, and headed at a brisk trot to rejoin her groom.

Would the dratted man forever haunt her? First he destroyed her sanctuary at the school. Then he turned up right next door to her, a jarring note to her London sojourn. Now he ruined her morning ride. The dreadful thought struck her that he might exercise his mount here every morning. If that were the case, she would just have to ride at a different time—or even find a different place. She had come to London to find a future for herself. She could hardly do that with him serving as a constant, painful reminder of the past.

She returned to the house shortly before nine to find Lady Xanthe awaiting her in the Gold Salon, an elegant little apartment on the ground floor. Her fairy godmother, she noted with an amusement that began to dispel her ill temper, had donned a vastly becoming carriage gown of rose-colored muslin. Phoebe paused in the doorway, admiring the effect.

"Well?" Xanthe demanded. "Do I look all the crack?"

"You do, indeed," Phoebe responded promptly. "Except you might want to make your wings invisible."

Xanthe arched her back, and the rounded wings

spread, flexed, then faded. A single oval feather drifted to the floor, its gilt edge sparkling. "I quite pride myself on my ability to dress appropriately."

Titus, whose plump form sprawled on the most comfortable chair the room boasted, voiced a low, staccato comment.

Xanthe threw him a reproachful look. "That was a costume affair, as I told you at the time. I was supposed to wear something unusual. And now, my dearest child," she went on, turning back to Phoebe, "are you ready for our morning's expedition?"

"I shall have to change first, though I am in a quake to visit a Bond Street *modiste* wearing a gown I made myself."

"Nonsense. You shall do neither." Xanthe smiled brightly at her, humming softly. After a moment, she said, "There. What do you think? And remember, it is only temporary."

Phoebe looked down, and found herself clad not in her ancient riding habit of faded black merino, but a morning gown of jaconet muslin with tiny puff sleeves and a wide flounce at the hem. "It is beautiful, ma'am," she breathed.

Xanthe beamed at her. "I thought you might like it. We shall order you a similar one."

Phoebe looked up, startled. "But there is no need! You have made such a lovely dress."

"But it will not last, my love. Anything wrought by my magic will fade once you have left London."

"I won't have need—" She broke off. She had no idea what she would need once she left London. If she were lucky enough to marry, she would indeed need a trousseau of sorts. If she were not lucky— The bleakness of the alternative chilled her.

"And what will you say when some envious young lady asks for the name of your *modiste?* No, my dear, you must be seen to order dresses." And with that, Xanthe swept them from the room.

Less than twenty minutes later, the fashionable barouche set them down before the exclusive establishment of Madame Bernadette. Less than twenty minutes after that, Phoebe heartily wished herself elsewhere. What, she wondered as the hands crept their slow journey around the clock, had ever persuaded her that a visit to a *modiste* of the first stare could be classified as one of the delights of a London Season? An experience, certainly. A delight, never. She had known that such an endeavor must necessarily involve the detailed discussion of the relative merits of various styles of sleeves and skirts, of trims and ribands and ruffles. Yet her reflections had grossly skimmed over the torture of standing for hour upon hour while seamstresses crawled about one, stabbing in pins, tucking, fitting, and exclaiming all the while that one had only to be a little patient and the job soon would be done.

As the noon hour came and went, they supplied her with tea and quite excellent sweet biscuits, but memories of the truly excellent meals conjured by Xanthe crept their wistful way into her thoughts. She could use a good, solid nuncheon. She also wouldn't mind sitting down.

The array of gauzes and muslins, silks and crepes she and Lady Xanthe had inspected left her quite dizzy, and the number of gowns her godmother deemed necessary to purchase, rather than merely conjure, horrified her. But to all of her objections, Lady Xanthe paid not the least heed. A walking dress of primrose muslin, a carriage dress of pale green merino, an evening dress of peach-colored silk and another of pale-blue crepe, even a riding habit of deep blue velvet, her godmother assured her, would be necessary for her no matter the outcome of her wish.

Which only served to remind her, once more, that this Season offered no certainties, only opportunities. And she had sworn to make the most of them. Well, why should she not meet someone she could love, and who could love her? That was, after all, the ultimate magic. And Xanthe's presence served as living, tangible proof that anything was possible.

Lady Xanthe tilted her head to one side and began to hum softly to herself, a rather pretty melody. She broke off abruptly and rose to her feet. "There, my love, we are quite finished for the day. Shall we go?"

Phoebe cast her a curious glance, but Xanthe's expression betrayed nothing but amused pleasure.

Leaving wasn't quite so simple, though. Last words had to be exchanged confirming the latest additions to their order, but finally the seamstresses gathered their pattern pieces, the lengths of cloth, and the list of Phoebe's measurements, and carried their burdens to the tables that lined the back walls. Madame Bernadette nodded in satisfaction, then once more picked up her notes to double check each of the decisions that had taken them all morning to reach.

At length, the *modiste* ushered them through the curtain and into the front room of her establishment.

They repeated their farewells, and Phoebe at last escaped into the bright, clear day and the early afternoon sun that filled Bruton Street. As she stood for a moment, welcoming the fresh air, the soft sound of Lady Xanthe's humming reached her, a scrap of tune that sounded familiar to Phoebe, though she couldn't quite place it.

Their barouche waited only a few steps away, but as Phoebe started toward it, a landaulet drew up behind. Its occupant, a tall woman just past middle age, of comfortable proportions and a decided flare for fashion, waved a cheery hand. "Lady Xanthe, what a delight to see you again. Is this your goddaughter?"

Xanthe took the woman's hand, then gestured for Phoebe to join them. She performed the introduction, adding, "Mrs. Mannering occupies one of the houses next to us in Half Moon Street, my dear."

"So we are neighbors." Mrs. Mannering beamed at her.

The woman, Phoebe decided, reminded her of a dumpling. A very fashionable one, of course, but a dumpling nevertheless. A softness characterized her features, and her eyes, neither quite blue nor quite gray, held a sentimental glow. One could smother in her comfortable air of coziness, yet one couldn't help but like her.

A sudden gleam lit Mrs. Mannering's eyes. "Lady Xanthe, you must come to dinner this evening. Say you will. Just potluck, you know. Nothing special. But it will give our girls a chance to become acquainted. I am chaperoning my niece for the Season, you see," she added to Phoebe.

Xanthe accepted with pleasure, and Phoebe with a secret thrill of delight. Her first party. It would be small, of course, probably consisting of only the four of them, but that didn't matter. It would be her *first*.

Mrs. Mannering accepted the hand of her footman to dismount from her carriage, repeated that she looked forward to seeing them that evening, and entered the establishment of Madame Bernadette. Xanthe watched her retreating figure and smiled that serene smile that spoke of mysteries and promises. After a moment she returned her attention to her surroundings and ushered Phoebe into their waiting barouche.

Phoebe sank back against the comfortable cushions with a sigh of pure pleasure, relieved to be sitting and not to have anyone crawling around her with a mouthful of pins. And tonight she would attend a dinner party, and wear not one of her serviceable merino gowns with their high necks and long sleeves, but something pretty that Xanthe would undoubtedly conjure just for the occasion. It would be a wonderful evening.

Lady Xanthe began to hum again, this time an unusual, haunting melody that made Phoebe think of twilight gardens in early summer, of moonlight cascading across still waters, of song birds trilling to their hearts' delight from the depths of flowering shrubs. Phoebe glanced at her, aware of the serenity of the ageless face—and the unquenchable humor of her violet eyes. In one of her pupils, Phoebe would have instantly suspected brewing mischief. In Lady Xanthe, it seemed twice as likely.

A fashionable barouche with a crest blazoned on its panel approached from the opposite direction, pulled by a pair of showy chestnuts. In the back sat a woman in a fur-trimmed pelisse and a modish, high poke bonnet, her haughty countenance wearing an expression of boredom. Lady Xanthe's humming increased in tempo for a moment, and the woman in the other carriage looked up, her gaze uncertain as it came to rest on them. Abruptly her face transformed into a radiant smile. "I shall send you a card for my musical *soiree,*" she called, and waved as the carriages separated in the traffic.

Phoebe craned to catch another glimpse of this generous personage, then turned to regard her godmother in a mixture of amusement and exasperation. "And who was that kind lady?"

"Lady Hessel." Xanthe's tone held mischievous satisfaction. "And I would not classify her as kind. She is excessively toplofty, but you won't mind that. You will meet only the most important people at her house."

"*I* am not one of the most important people," Phoebe pointed out.

Xanthe shook her head, that smile of secret enjoyment more pronounced. "If you weren't, then you wouldn't be invited, now would you, my dear?"

"She wasn't inviting me. She was inviting you. And since I heard you humming, I am tolerably certain she has never laid eyes on you before."

Xanthe straightened, regarding her with offended dignity. "I would never try to influence someone against their will. That would be quite wrong in me.

Besides," she added, tilting her head to one side, sudden laughter dancing in her eyes, "it is not really conjuring if someone responds to an idea that is floating about, is it? I never impressed it upon her, after all."

"No, of course you did not." Phoebe regarded her in fascination. "Nor did you seek to influence Mrs. Mannering. The idea is utterly preposterous."

Xanthe's smile deepened. "I am so glad you understand."

"Of course I do. It is the most natural thing in the world for a complete stranger—and a very important one, at that—to know who we are and invite us to her very select gathering. I daresay it happens to every young lady making her curtsy to society."

"Well, how can you possibly meet any eligible gentlemen if you never go anywhere or do anything?" Xanthe settled back in the carriage. "Do you know, we have yet to actually attend a party, but I find I am already enjoying myself immensely."

"That is because you were not the one being fitted." A ragged sigh escaped Phoebe. "I fear I shall simply fall asleep this evening and quite ruin Mrs. Mannering's dinner party."

Xanthe patted her hand. "Never mind, my love. You may lie down for a while when we get home."

"I thought we were to go to Grafton House."

Xanthe made a dismissive gesture. "The most knowledgeable people, it seems, go in the morning. Tomorrow morning, in fact," she added after a moment's reflection, "for you must have several pairs of silk stockings and a shawl before tomorrow night, and I do so hate to waste magic on such trifles."

Phoebe brightened at this mention of a second invitation. "Where do we go?"

"A card party at Arnsdale House. You shall like it excessively, I promise you. And it will give you the opportunity to meet some more people. I suppose," she added thoughtfully, "we ought to present you at Court."

Presentation at Court. Phoebe leaned her head back against the squabs. It didn't seem real. None of this seemed real. Xanthe knew unerringly the best shops. Other ladies, wealthy ones with prominent titles, gave way to her. People whose names Phoebe had heard her pupils whisper with awe bowed and waved to Xanthe. It seemed not a single door in London would remain shut to them.

Even, Phoebe wondered with a sudden flicker of anticipation, that holiest of holies, Almack's? She couldn't let herself believe that might be possible, not after the way her pupils had always spoken of it in hushed accents. No, there was no likelihood of it. No matter what magical capabilities Lady Xanthe might possess, Phoebe remained a penniless Nobody, lacking so much as a single relative who might make her acceptable to the lofty patronesses.

"Lady Sefton," pronounced Xanthe in an offhanded tone, "has promised to send you vouchers for Almack's. Should you like that, my love?"

Phoebe opened her mouth, closed it again, then managed, "How?"

Xanthe laughed, a delightful, musical sound. "I promised you a Season, did I not? It couldn't possibly be complete without a visit to Almack's."

"But *how?*" Phoebe repeated. "I may never have been to London before, but I know a great deal about society; and for me to go to Almack's—it is simply impossible. I'm a Nobody! No mere *suggestion* could accomplish that."

"You may tell me so again, three weeks from Wednesday night, when you are to make your first appearance."

Phoebe leaned her head back against the squabs. Xanthe was more than living up to her part of the covenant. Phoebe would be given every opportunity to meet any number of eligible gentlemen, and leaders of society, at that, with sufficient wealth to consider Thomas's expenses trifling. But would she be able to fulfill her part? Would any of them be seized by the desire to make her his wife? And if by chance any one was, would she desire to *become* his wife?

This was no time for missishness, she reminded herself. Xanthe had granted her this one and only Season. If she wasted it, her future loomed bleak. So she couldn't waste it. If she were so fortunate as to receive an offer, she could not afford to reject it. And why should she not receive one? she rallied herself. Anything seemed possible when Lady Xanthe hummed her magical tunes.

By the time the barouche at last turned onto Half Moon Street, they had received two more invitations, both for balls. And before each invitation, Xanthe had hummed one of her mysterious, mesmerizing melodies. Not influencing people, of course, Phoebe reminded herself, smiling at Xanthe's rationalization.

Merely putting suggestions out where they might be intercepted and acted upon.

As they drew up before the house, the door opened at once, and Arthur, the senior footman, hurried down to hand them from the carriage. Phoebe paused to glance at the neighboring house just to the left. "Is that where Mrs. Mannering lives?"

Xanthe turned back from the door. "There? Oh, no, dear. The other side."

"The other—" Phoebe broke off. "The other side. *Directly* next door to us?"

"That's right, my love. She is chaperoning her niece. I believe you know the girl, Miss Lucilla Saunderton? She and her brother arrived in town only the day before we did."

Phoebe stared at the neighboring front door, aghast. First the man destroyed her security. Then he turned up on her doorstep, next ruined her morning ride. Now, it seemed, as she took her first faltering steps into the polite world, she was to once more trip over Sir Miles Saunderton.

"It won't be easy for her," Xanthe informed Titus, who sprawled in the center of her bed, industriously bathing the long white fur of his stomach. She set her bonnet on the top of a dresser, hummed a snatch of a tune, then examined the rather fetching lace cap trimmed with blue ribands that appeared in her hands. "Poor child, she's so determined that her head shall rule her heart."

The tip of Titus's tail twitched.

Xanthe frowned. "But that's just the point. When one is strong-willed and independent like that, it makes it very difficult to trust one's emotions. She's more than half inclined not to trust even me, you know," she added as she set the lacy confection on her mass of fair hair.

Titus paused in his ablutions, fixed her with a meaningful eye, and uttered a series of staccato sounds.

Xanthe, who could see him in the mirror as she tied the ribands in a jaunty bow beneath one ear, fixed him with a reproving frown. "High-handed? Me? I know better than to thrust people into what is best for them. She'll discover it on her own. We have the entire Season."

Titus rolled his considerable bulk to the side and swished his tail.

Xanthe eyed him with fond exasperation. "That's easy enough for you to think, isn't it? I just hope you realize how much work we have to do. If people are to 'discover' things, they quite often need a little help. It always amazes me how blind to the obvious they can be." She returned her attention to her own reflection. "A Court presentation means hoops, I suppose," she muttered in disgust.

A deep, contented purr sounded from behind her.

She shot a forbidding look at the self-satisfied cat. "You needn't be so smug just because you don't have to rig yourself out in a ridiculous getup. There's plenty for you to do, as well. And you're shedding on my bed," she added as a parting shot as she headed for the door.

Four

Sir Miles Saunderton cast a rapid, assessing glance over his reflection, and nodded in satisfaction. Nothing out of place, nothing out of the ordinary. More from habit than necessity he adjusted a fold in his neck-cloth, then turned from the cheval glass.

His valet, who stood a few paces away before the fire that heated the room against the chill of the evening, eyed him with the air of one bent upon doing his duty despite a high probability of failure. Miles fought back a touch of sudden amusement and with an effort kept it from showing. "Is something the matter, Vines?" he inquired.

The aging servitor, who had been in Miles's employ since first he'd needed the services of a gentleman's gentleman, fixed him with a reproachful frown. "You know Miss Lucy has requested that you wear your emerald pin in your cravat, Master Miles. And that heavy fob that was your late father's."

"She has requested a great many things of me over the years," Miles said with a note of apology, "and very few of them have been suitable. Some of them," he added with an air of reminiscence, "were hardly polite."

"Now, Master Miles, you know how Miss Lucy gets when she's out of temper."

Which seemed to be most of the time of late, Miles reflected, but kept that thought to himself.

"She doesn't mean a word of it," Vines continued. "But there's nothing to take exception at over this request, nor would it do any harm to humor her."

That stopped Miles. "What," he demanded, "do you know about tonight that I do not?"

Vines adopted an air of injured innocence that wouldn't have fooled even someone less well acquainted with him than Miles. "I'm sure I don't know what you can mean, sir."

"Cut line, Vines. Has my sister unearthed another dashing female to throw at my head?"

A pained expression replaced the innocence. "I do wish you would not express yourself in so vulgar a manner, sir. What your late father—"

"My late father would be wholly in sympathy, and so you know it. *Am* I to have some eligible female thrust upon me tonight?"

"I really couldn't say, sir." Vines sought refuge in brushing his master's coat, an entirely unnecessary operation, for he had done so already. As he reached the front, a heavy golden chain appeared in his hand as if by magic, and he tried to hook one end through a button hole of Miles's waistcoat. One glance at his master's reproving face, though, and he abandoned the attempt.

"Just so," said Miles as his man backed away.

Vines emitted a sound perilously close to a sniff. "It would do you no harm to add a touch of dash to your appearance, sir."

Miles regarded his man in exasperation. "I have every intention of marrying, Vines. I am even— though my aunt and sister do not credit it—looking about me for a suitable wife. So far, I have discovered not one single female whose conversation I could bear for more than half an hour at a time." And with that, he strode out of the room.

He had no need to hurry, of course; when he entered the salon, he found that neither his aunt nor Lucilla had yet come downstairs. He crossed to the occasional table where the decanters stood, poured out a large glass of Madeira, and went to stand before the fire while he drank it. He had told Vines the truth—more or less. At one-and-thirty, it was high time he set up his nursery, and he knew it. But finding a female who could inspire him to become a tenant for life was proving difficult.

He had met any number of eligible ladies, each possessed of intelligent conversation, grace, and a measure of beauty. Yet with not one of them had he experienced that sense of having found a kindred spirit. And that, he deemed, was the most necessary element in choosing a life's partner.

He had helped his sister Amelia find the right gentleman. She had longed for political importance, and the middle-aged diplomat, destined for a peerage in the very near future, had suited her to perfection. Harry—God rest his soul—had been army-mad since a youth, and never so much as looked at a lady until

Miles had pointed out the plain, adoring Isabel who lived on the adjoining estate. The girl had thrilled at the chance to follow the drum with her beloved husband. Juliana had dreamed of social—and sartorial—prominence. He had introduced her to a member of Brummel's set, who had elevated her to the elite as one of society's leading hostesses. His sister Susanna, always independent, had found the naval captain he presented to her exactly to her liking, not minding his extended absences, but always delighting in his returns. All happy marriages, all based on mutual interests and temperaments.

And then there was Lucilla. His youngest sister talked of love, with that starry-eyed enchantment of one who hadn't the faintest understanding about which she spoke. At seventeen, the girl didn't yet know the difference between a lasting emotion and a far more fleeting, if intense, infatuation. Somehow, he had to find her a suitable husband—one who could make her happy, one who could handle her—before she ruined herself with her outrageous behavior.

The door opened behind him, and he dragged his gaze from the flames to see his sister standing on the threshold, eyeing him with disapprobation. "You are late," he pointed out, but with a smile, as this was the norm.

She wrinkled her nose. "Was it worth it? Do you like my new gown?"

In truth, he hadn't really noticed it. But recalled to a sense of brotherly duty, he duly admired the half robe of white gauze, open down the front to reveal a white muslin underdress threaded through with green ribands. "Very pretty."

"Pretty!" she cried. "Miles, you are a beast! It's perfectly beautiful, and just the thing for dinner with our neighbors, do you not think?"

Actually, he hadn't given the matter any thought whatsoever. He knew his own rig to be suitable, but the intricacies of female apparel—and their apparent enjoyment in discussing it in minute detail—escaped him. He fell back on a tested and assured response. "I stand corrected. You look delightful."

Lucy beamed on him and ran forward, grasping his hands. "Thank you. You can be the dearest of brothers when you set your mind to it."

The implication, that he could also be the vilest, did not need to be spoken between them. That discussion had taken place during the journey to town, and involved the names of more than one half-pay lieutenant and a variety of clandestine meetings that would have resulted in a shocking scandal had he not removed her swiftly first from their home in Surrey, and then from Bath. Lucy was already proving more of a handful than his other three sisters combined.

Why in blazes did the girl have to pine after opportunists and fortune hunters? A young gentleman every bit as dashing and romantic as Lucy could wish lived right at her doorstep, yet the eyes of long familiarity throughout childhood blinded her to the charms other young ladies noted in an instant. If she didn't wake up soon, Lord Ashby might well drop the handkerchief elsewhere.

"You aren't wearing Papa's fob!" she cried. "Oh,

Miles, you can be so very vexatious. When I particularly asked Vines to make sure you looked your best."

"He tried. What makes you think I shall like this female you've found?"

Lucy's eyes widened, and she looked away at once. "Why, whatever can you mean? What female?"

His deep chuckle escaped him. "I'm too old a dog to be fooled by such tricks, my dear. Who is she?"

Her breath escaped her in a rush. "Oh, Miles, I have not so much as laid eyes upon her yet, but Aunt Jane thinks she may be the very thing! She is quite old— over twenty, she assured me—and she says that this lady regards one in the most straightforward manner, and all the while there is laughter lurking in her eyes. Just like you."

"I don't suppose you would believe me if I told you I would prefer to find a wife on my own?"

"Yes, but you aren't even trying." She tilted her head to one side. "You've never shown the least interest in any of the ladies Juliana and Amelia and even Susanna have found for you, and several of them have been diamonds of the first water. You only speak to the most docile of females, who are quite beyond their last prayers and utterly boring into the bargain."

"And what, my dear Lucy, would you know about docility?" he asked, nettled by her assessment.

"Pray do not be vexatious, dear Miles," she said in a voice that perfectly mimicked her eldest sister Amelia in an exasperated mood.

"Minx." He caught himself before he tousled her hair. That she had delighted in his doing just that when she was seven had nothing whatsoever to do with her preferences now that she was elevated from the schoolroom. Now it would be unforgivable.

A heartfelt sigh escaped Lucy. "Oh, I do wish Juliana were not mired in the country with her sweet new baby, or that Amelia could have come to town sooner, or Susanna were not in the family way. They would have known just how to—" She broke off.

Before Miles could demand just what it was his other three sisters would have known how to do, Mrs. Mannering hurried into the room, draped in ells of lavender gauze, her hair festooned with matching ostrich plumes. She set them all to plumping cushions already plumped, checking decanters already filled, and generally subjecting them to a fit of nerves at her first dinner party of the year. Miles pressed her firmly but kindly into a seat and presented her with a glass of negus. Just as she seemed about to relax, the knocker sounded on the door, and she sprang once more to her feet.

"They are here!" she exclaimed, quite unnecessarily. She cast a rapid glance over Lucilla, then turned her attention to Miles. "Dear boy," she said, "you will be an attentive host, will you not?"

"When have I ever failed you?" With the ease of practice, he fended off her misplaced attempts to straighten his immaculate neckcloth.

He turned as the door into the salon opened, and found himself facing a handsome woman of middle years, just above average height, with pale hair and violet eyes, gowned in a becoming blue silk of exquisite cut and design. The material rustled softly as she glided forward, hands extended to greet Aunt Jane.

"How glad I am you could come." Aunt Jane kissed her cheek. "Dear Lady Xanthe. And Miss Caldicot."

Miss Caldicot. With a surge of unholy delight, Miles saw the petite figure who stood rigidly a little behind Lady Xanthe. Nothing could exceed the haughty indifference of her features, but antipathy welled out from her, as tangible as if it had solid form. Good God, had she known where she was going before she accepted? He doubted it very much. He could sympathize with the position in which she found herself, but he intended to enjoy it nonetheless.

"Miss Caldicot!" Lucy rushed forward, hands extended. "Oh, my dearest Miss Caldicot! Whatever are you doing here? Aunt Jane, is *she* the one you told me about? Oh, how droll! I never guessed it could possibly be my own dear Miss Caldicot."

"You are acquainted?" faltered Mrs. Mannering, looking from one to the other.

"Dear Aunt Jane, Miss Caldicot is—was—quite my favorite of my instructresses. But whatever has brought you up to London? You said not a word about it."

"Like you, I am to enjoy the Season." The soft, musical voice conveyed the utmost confidence, the air of one in complete control.

It didn't fool Miles. He could admire her manner— in fact, the more he saw of her, the more he found to admire—but he could sense her underlying uneasiness. He approved her ability to disguise it.

"You must allow me to present my nephew—" Mrs. Mannering broke off in uncertainty. "That is, unless you have also met?"

"I have not had the pleasure." Lady Xanthe held out her hand. "How do you do, Sir Miles?"

Miles made a leg, and found himself the subject of a rather amused scrutiny. His own humor welled, and it was with difficulty that he turned a relatively sober countenance upon her companion. "Miss Caldicot I am acquainted with, though we have never been properly introduced. A pleasure, as always, Miss Caldicot."

Her eyes, an intriguing shade of misty gray, flashed in what could only be sheer animosity. "You can have no idea how I have looked forward to it," she said, with a dryness only he could appreciate.

His smile broadened. "Counting the moments, to be sure," he said softly, so only she would hear.

"Until we leave," she murmured in the same tone. Her polite smile belied the acidity of her words.

Lucy, despite engaging in polite conversation with Lady Xanthe, had cast frequent, furtive glances in their direction while they spoke. Now, with all the air of one who could no longer contain her curiosity, she joined them, taking Miss Caldicot's arm and drawing her toward the sofa. "Pray, tell me how this has come about," she begged.

So, his littlest sister entertained hopes that he and her former instructress might develop a *tendre* for one another. Miss Caldicot would shortly set her straight on that account, he felt certain. He watched them, noting Lucy's respect and obvious affection for her former preceptress, and noting Miss Caldicot's air of good breeding in the face of this adversity.

He also noted the profuse amounts of her coppery brown hair drawn up to the back of her head from where it cascaded to her shoulders in a riot of curls. He much preferred it to the rather austere chignon he'd seen her wear before. This style enhanced the delicacy of her features, the large, wide-set eyes, the retroussé nose—and the very determined chin. He had noted her elegant carriage before; now she wore a gown suited to it. He knew himself to be no expert on ladies' fashions, but he found her half robe of sea foam green gauze, open over an underdress of white silk, to be attractive in the extreme.

Abruptly, and not quite sure why, he said, "I trust the remainder of your ride this morning was less eventful, Miss Caldicot."

"Ride?" Lucy looked from one to the other of them. "Miles, you never said anything about encountering her. And what was so eventful about it?"

Miss Caldicot's eyes kindled. "Your brother staged the most dashing of rescues, but I fear I was wholly unappreciative. You see, he believed my mount to be bolting with me, when in fact I merely indulged in a gallop."

Lucilla fixed him with a withering eye. "Really, Miles, if that isn't just like you! You are forever jumping in and fishing people out of troubles, even when they don't want your aid."

"Oh, Lucy, pray—" Her aunt regarded her in dismay. "Miles is such a gentleman, any lady must be delighted to be rescued by him. And, dear Miss Caldicot, what a perfectly startling experience it must have been for you. Quite unpleasant, I fear. I do trust my nephew apologized."

Had he? Miles couldn't remember, but he rather

doubted it. He'd been enjoying himself too much. But Miss Caldicot said all that was proper, winning a smile from his aunt and a rolling-eyed grimace from his sister, who promptly drew Miss Caldicot back into an earnest conversation. Miles poured glasses of ratafia for their guests and engaged Lady Xanthe in polite small talk. His gaze, though, returned frequently to his sister and her companion.

Lucilla laughed, cast a mischievous look over her shoulder at him, and turned back to Miss Caldicot, speaking rapidly in a voice so low he could barely make out the sound. Minx, he reflected. Probably matchmaking with a vengeance. He'd take her to task for it at the first opportunity—if Miss Caldicot did not beat him to it.

Chievers, their butler for as long as Miles could remember, announced dinner, and Miles escorted Lady Xanthe up the stairs to the dining room on the first floor at the back of the house. The other ladies followed, and he seated them, Lady Xanthe on his right and Miss Caldicot on his left, with Lucy just beyond her. Lady Xanthe at once turned her attention to his aunt, which left him to regard his other partner.

As the host, he knew it behooved him not to provoke her. The impulse, though, to draw her into another argument and enjoy her indignation proved almost irresistible. But resist it he did. He set down his glass of burgundy and fixed her with a conciliatory smile. "I believe I must thank you for not denouncing me as an unprincipled meddler after this morning's *contretemps.*"

Miss Caldicot looked up at him over the rim of her

own goblet, her large eyes holding a considering expression. "Amazing restraint on my part, did you not think?" she agreed with false sweetness.

"Most amazing." So much for the offering of olive branches. "I suppose my sister has been reinforcing your low opinion of me?"

Again that sweet smile. "There is absolutely no need for that, I assure you."

Irritation stirred in him; but before he could speak, one of the footmen appeared at his shoulder, and he held his tongue until the man had finished placing several slices of salmon, swimming in a rich cream sauce, on his plate. The conversation became general, and he did not find an opportunity to speak to her with any degree of privacy until they had retired to the drawing room, where Lucilla seated herself at the pianoforte to show off some of the skills drilled into her by Miss Caldicot's persistence.

Miles drew up a chair near his guest and considered her austere expression. Seldom had he encountered a lady less desirous of being pleased. And seldom, he admitted to himself, had he encountered one he would so much like to please. Just why, he couldn't be certain. Perhaps it had something to do with the proud carriage of her head, or the delightfully melodic timbre of her laugh, or maybe the independence she wore as armor. Before he could explore the matter more thoroughly, though, he had to settle a little matter between them.

"Miss Caldicot," he said softly, so as not to attract the attention of his aunt or Lady Xanthe.

Miss Caldicot kept her gaze on Lucilla and made no answer.

Stubborn, he reflected. If she weren't so angry with him, and if he weren't so determined to end their feud, he would find that trait amusing. He tried again, this time without preamble. "You persist in blaming me for something for which I am not responsible."

"Indeed?" Just that one, cold word. She still did not look at him.

"I never suggested you should lose your position. In fact, I never mentioned your name."

She turned the penetrating regard of her fine, mist-colored eyes upon him. "But you did reprimand the Misses Crippenham for not keeping a sufficiently watchful eye upon your sister, did you not?"

"Would not you have done the same, had our positions been reversed?"

This time, her look held nothing but withering contempt. "I suppose you believe it to be a very simple matter to know, at every single moment, the whereabouts of fifteen girls? And before you say I should check on them even after they have retired to their beds, I can only ask how you think I discovered her missing in the first place!"

"Your dismissal was wholly unjust," he agreed.

She opened her eyes to their widest and said, with no attempt to veil her sarcasm, "I cannot tell you how much it means to me to hear you say that."

"I shall say so to the Misses Crippenham if you should wish it," he offered.

"I do not!" came her sharp response. "I have had

quite enough of your interference, thank you." She rose and went to sit beside Lady Xanthe.

She proved a challenge, he reflected. And it was one he intended to meet—and defeat. He could always concoct some scheme by which he could place himself in her good graces, but she would undoubtedly consider that further evidence of his interfering. He would have to give the matter some thought.

Miles had not yet arrived at any viable plan for melting Miss Caldicot's anger by the following evening. His tentative ideas concerning an early morning ride in the park had been nipped in the bud by the simple fact she had not put in an appearance. That had disappointed him more than he'd expected. He indulged Cuthbert, his raw-boned roan, in a reprehensible gallop, and regretted she had not been there to see; he very much would have enjoyed her outrage after the lecture he had given her for just such behavior.

He did not see her again until that night, when he escorted his aunt and sister to the Arnsdales' card party. A crowd of people already filled the rooms, and the hum of voices assaulted him as soon as he stepped through the door. And the Season, he reminded himself ruefully, had barely begun. He greeted his hostess, then ushered the ladies in his care into the rooms beyond.

Lucilla, gowned in a rather becoming creation of white muslin, festooned with a score or more of pink riband knots and roses, hurried forward, eyes wide and eager. Her first party, Miles reflected. He would have his hands full, the little minx.

Still following the girl, he strode into the next drawing room and looked about. Miss Caldicot, he noted with a surprising touch of pleasure, stood on the far side of the room, a tiny figure quite overshadowed by the tall gentleman of fashion at her side. Miles's gaze narrowed. Not just any gentleman. She captivated Lord Arnsdale himself, that notorious dandy and connoisseur of the ladies. Quite a feather in her cap, to keep him at her side. But then he'd already discovered that she possessed a wit and intelligence commensurate with her undeniable beauty. Apparently, she had charmed their host.

He found he worked his way toward them, exchanging polite greetings with acquaintances without really noticing whom he passed. Miss Caldicot, he noted with an odd mixture of pleasure and something he couldn't quite identify, was decidedly in looks. The pale-blue crepe of her gown set off the copper highlights in her hair, which clustered in becoming ringlets about her face. She stood very straight, very proud. It was no wonder Arnsdale regarded her with that— that *damned* lecherous expression.

He slowed, gripped by a sudden new problem. How did one warn a lady with whom one was not upon terms about the man? Or for that matter, about any number of seducers and libertines who cluttered the *ton*? She would never listen to a word he uttered.

He glanced back, looking for Lucy, and his brow snapped down. She stood somewhat aside from the other guests with a dashing young lieutenant resplendent in scarlet regimentals, gazing up into his face with an idiotish expression on her own. Damn the girl, he couldn't take his eyes off her for two minutes without her discovering some half-pay officer with whom to flirt.

He strode up to them, awarded the young man a distant bow, and turned to Lucy. "Have you paid your respects to Miss Caldicot, yet?" he inquired in a tone from which he kept his vexation.

"Oh, has she arrived already?" She sounded distracted, and her gaze returned at once to her companion.

Miles took her arm. "It would not do to be backward about such things, my dear." He directed a dismissive nod to the officer and drew Lucy away. "Who was that?" he asked, still trying to keep his voice noncommittal.

"Oh, is he not the most handsome man you have ever seen?" breathed Lucy. She looked up at Miles, her eyes glowing.

His heart sank. "I cannot consider myself an expert."

"Well, he is," she declared. "And so very charming. Oh, Miles, I am so happy you brought me to town."

Miles, at the moment, felt quite the opposite. With admirable restraint, he said merely, "I am glad you are enjoying yourself," and led her toward her former instructress.

As they approached, he had the dubious pleasure of seeing Arnsdale kiss Miss Caldicot's hand, then walk away. Lucy hurried forward, her hands extended, and greeted her former instructress with delight. Miss

Caldicot turned, and Miles clearly saw the glow in her lovely eyes. Apparently, the earl's gallantries were much to her liking. He could only regret her taste. But the glow faded as her gaze came to rest on him, and once more he faced the cool, composed Miss Caldicot. She greeted Lucy with warmth, himself with restraint, and excused herself promptly to go to one of the card rooms.

Lucy watched her retreating figure. "What a perfectly delightful idea. I believe I, too, shall play at cards. It cannot be too difficult to find a partner."

Something in the airiness with which she spoke put Miles instantly upon the alert. He followed, until a familiar voice, calling his name, caught his attention. He turned to find himself facing a young gentleman whose impeccable attire, muscular build, and tanned features proclaimed him a Corinthian. "Ashby!" he declared in real pleasure, and strode forward to take the hand of his Surrey neighbor. "What are you doing in town so early? I thought you were settled in Leicestershire until May."

"I came back for my cousin's wedding, and figured I might as well stay." He turned to regard the crowded room in distaste. "What brings you here?"

"Lucy. Finally found a chaperon for her. My Aunt Jane Mannering."

Ashby brightened. "Finished at that boarding school at last, has she? Must be in high gig. Is she here?"

Miles started to escort him to find Lucy, but an elderly matron gowned in mauve satin, with a piercing voice and a gimlet eye, hailed the baron. Miles recognized her as one of Ashby's numerous relations and gave him up for lost for the next quarter of an hour. Adjuring his friend to join him in the card room when he should disentangle himself, he set forth to see what Lucy was about.

She wasn't in the first salon he entered. Neither was Miss Caldicot. At least they might be together—though he held out no real hope his sister would behave any better for her former instructress than she did for anyone else.

He entered the next room, only to be brought to a halt by a hauntingly familiar laugh, low and musical, so compelling he wanted to join in. Miss Caldicot. He scanned the room, then spotted her only two tables from the door. Her partner seemed to be entertaining her very well, he noted. He moved forward a step, and found she sat across the table from Viscount Wolverhampton, an amiable peer a trifle too inclined toward the petticoat line. In fact, the man could be an unconscionable flirt. On the whole, Miles could not consider any gentleman with so dubious a reputation to be a suitable companion for a young lady as innocent as he deemed Miss Caldicot to be.

"Is that not the little Saunderton chit?" asked a woman's voice behind him.

He glanced about to see a haughty dame of advancing years, her lorgnette leveled across the room. She had set off an elaborate gown of amber satin with a head of ostrich feathers dyed to match. Diamonds, every bit as famous as the lady herself, gleamed about the neck of Lady Grieves.

Her companion, the equally daunting Lady Templeton, raised her own lorgnette. "Do you mean that rather pretty girl with the officer?"

Lady Grieves gave an affected laugh. "Of course with an officer, my dear Amanda. One hears such rumors."

"Tell me!" demanded Lady Templeton, all agog for the latest *on dit*.

"It seems she has been seen in Bath, in the Sydney Gardens. Clandestine meetings, one must suppose." She dropped her lorgnette and lowered her voice, though it retained its carrying quality. "And always officers, it is said."

Miles clenched his teeth to keep from directing a much needed setdown to Lady Grieves. It would do Lucy irremediable harm if he came to points with two of society's undisputed leaders. He would simply have to steer the girl away from anyone in a red coat for the next two months.

He wended his way through the tables until he reached Lucy's. She glanced up at him, and her eyes took on a wary expression. She knew perfectly well he didn't approve, the little minx. For that matter, judging from the uneasy glance of her companion— the same officer to whom she'd been speaking earlier—his irritation must be clear to read on his face. With an effort, he forced his countenance to betray nothing more than civil politeness. He awarded an acknowledging nod to the officer, then turned to the girl. "I need to speak with you, Lucy."

Her features set in a rebellious glower. "I am playing piquet, Miles."

"You would oblige me by coming with me. If you

will excuse us?" he added to her officer as he caught her elbow and drew her to her feet.

"I will go nowhere with you when you are being so disagreeable!" Lucy hissed at him.

"You will come at once if you wish to avoid a scandal."

"Scandal?" Lucy's voice squeaked on the word.

He drew her, no longer protesting, from the room and into a smaller chamber that had been closed off for the evening. He put his hand on her shoulder, leaning close so that what he said would be for her ears alone. In a few well-chosen words, he warned her of the conversation between the two influential ladies.

Lucy listened in silence, her eyes growing wider by the moment. When he finished, she pulled away, tears brimming on her lashes. "How—how could they! No, I cannot believe it. You are making the whole of it up. You are quite hateful."

He regarded her in a mixture of exasperation and sympathy. "It is far too easy to gain a reputation for being fast—however unjust it might be."

She sniffed, and the tears threatened to spill down her cheeks. "It is all so dreadfully unfair."

"It is also the way of the world." Miles frowned at her.

She blanched. "But I have not compromised myself. To even suggest such a thing is vastly unkind."

"No, you have not, yet. And if you will come with me, I believe we may undo some of the damage by—"

She pulled away. "You are just trying to be managing, and I won't have it!" She turned on her heel, only to come to an abrupt halt as she almost collided with the tiny figure of Miss Caldicot, who stood just inside the doorway.

Her former instructress directed an icy glare at Miles. "At least you had the decency to draw her into another room before raking her over the coals. But did it not occur to you how singular it must look when it is seen that she has been crying? No, return to the others. I feel certain we shall do much better without you."

And with that, he found himself firmly closed out of the room.

Five

To Phoebe's intense relief, Lucy did not break down in tears. She compelled the girl to sit upon a sofa, but though Lucy sniffed a few times, she soon regained her composure. She dabbed at her eyes with a hand-kerchief and pronounced herself to be much better.

"He just will meddle so in what is, after all, *my* life. Oh, Miss Caldicot, I have met the most wonderful gentleman! Any lady must be thrilled to have captured his attention. And here is Miles, making any excuse he can find to prevent me from speaking with him."

"Is that why he brought you in here just now?"

Her color heightened. "He said the most dreadful things to me. How could I possibly cause a scandal just by playing cards with Lieutenant Harwich?"

"He told you people are talking about you and other officers?"

Lucy stared at her aghast. "Do you mean it is true? You have heard those horrible rumors as well? Oh, it is so unfair!"

"But you must see why it is unwise for you to be seen with another officer just at this moment," Phoebe pointed out gently.

"But Lieutenant Harwich is different!" Lucy looked up, a smile trembling on her lips. "Oh, Miss Caldicot, he is so very wonderful," she rushed on as if the floodgates had been released. "I knew the moment I laid eyes on him I should love him forever. And it is exactly the same with him!"

"But—" Phoebe broke off, trying to sort out her thoughts. "This is not the same officer you met at—"

"No! No, of course not. I met Lieutenant Harwich tonight. Lieutenant Gregory Harwich."

"I see." Phoebe considered this with no little concern. "And you knew at once?"

Lucy nodded, her eyes glowing. "Is it not the most romantic thing you ever dreamed of?"

"Unexpected, certainly. But in my experience, passions so quickly begun usually die just as fast."

"Not this one," Lucy averred. "You must help me, my dear Miss Caldicot. Miles will listen to you. You can make him understand I shall never love anyone else."

Phoebe hesitated, picking her words with care. "I don't believe your brother and I are on such terms that anything I might say would carry any weight with him."

Dismay filled Lucy's mobile countenance. "Promise me you will try," she cried, and continued her begging until Phoebe at last agreed to speak with her brother.

Of course, Phoebe reflected as she set forth upon her distasteful errand, she had made no commitment to Lucy about what she would actually say to Miles. Only that she would speak to him about his sister.

She worked her way into the main drawing room,

then searched through the Fashionables who spilled out into the adjoining rooms. When Xanthe had first spoken of a card party, Phoebe had imagined a small gathering, perhaps ten people in all. But she must have counted more than fifty.

She at last spotted Sir Miles on the far side of one of the card salons. He was easy to pick out; his restrained elegance showed in marked contrast to the excesses of the Tulips and Pinks. Only a single fob crossed the subdued brocade of his waistcoat, and the ruby signet ring on his hand was not the least bit ostentatious, as were so many she had seen. She had only to look for broad shoulders set off by a superbly cut coat, and the muscled frame that must always proclaim him a Corinthian. Memory flooded through her, of being lifted in those strong arms from her precarious perch atop an iron rail, of the feel of his fingers tight about her waist, of his air of amused confidence. . . . Her cheeks burned.

At the moment, he conversed with a rather pretty lady just past the bloom of youth, but by no means marred by age. Their discussion seemed serious—or at least solemn—and Phoebe hesitated to intrude. A certain understanding seemed to exist between the two, as though they had known one another for a long time. Or perhaps it indicated something more?

Curiosity welled in her, and she watched the lady covertly. She could detect no signs of humor in her docile eyes. In fact, the lady didn't seem at all suited to the lively humor that all too often overcame Sir Miles. But then perhaps he preferred a companion of a less lively turn of mind. She probably accepted—or even welcomed—his meddling in her affairs. Phoebe doubted an argument had ever sprung up between them.

She turned away, and almost collided with a gentleman who had been walking at right angles to her. To her consternation, she found herself staring at an elaborate brocade waistcoat shot through with gold thread, and a coat of deep mulberry velvet. Her gaze traveled upward, past an impeccably tied cravat boasting a sapphire stick pin, into the handsome, tanned face of the Marquis of Rushmere.

Rushmere. Phoebe stared at him, disoriented to see him here, so far from the Misses Crippenham's Academy in Bath. But so many things had changed since last she'd seen him there. . . .

He stared back. His expression of polite boredom faded behind a confident smile, which in turn faded into a puzzled crease in his brow. "Do you know," he said with the smile that had caused her former pupils to whisper his name in awe, "I feel certain we have been introduced, yet I cannot imagine how I could have forgotten the name of any lady so lovely."

He delivered the line with practiced ease, but that didn't detract from its charm in the least, she decided. She smiled back. "We have indeed met, my lord."

A gleam lit his eyes. "Then, I may claim you for a game of cards without the least impropriety. If you will grant me the pleasure?" He offered his arm.

"I cannot guarantee my ability will please you."

"Sometimes," he asserted in heart-melting tones, "the company more than makes up for the game."

Another delightful line. But this one, too, sounded

like the type a practiced flirt kept in his repertoire. Phoebe placed her fingers on his sleeve, flattered and not a little smug that he should bother to make her the object of his gallantries. For one reprehensible moment, she wished Miss Georgeana Middleton, or Lady Jane Hatchard, could see her now, strolling off so casually with their idol. It quite set her up in her own conceit.

Of course, if she were honest with herself—as she had a disconcerting tendency to be—she had to admit she could not think of a single reason why the marquis should single her out in so flattering a manner. Unless . . .

Xanthe. Had her fairy godmother released another of her "suggestions" in the marquis's vicinity?

She allowed him to seat her at an empty table for two, and as he broke the seal on a fresh pack and sorted out the lower pips, she cast a surreptitious look about for Xanthe. And there she sat close by, indulging in a rather peculiar game of silver loo. Peculiar, of course, in that Xanthe's wagers floated several inches above the cloth, and not one of the other players seemed to notice that her coins rainbowed through a sparkling array of color, or that the size of her cards shifted with carefree abandon.

Xanthe, it appeared, was enjoying herself. Did she intend for Phoebe to do so, also? Or had she some greater purpose in mind? A nobleman of Rushmere's rank would not pay attention to a penniless ex-schoolmistress without a little outside influence.

As the marquis dealt, she considered the possibilities. Rushmere had been the epitome of her students' dreams for so long, the object of their gossip and sighs, she had come to include him in a few daydreams of her own. Had Xanthe known this when she gifted Phoebe with a wish for a husband? And if so, was Rushmere more than a confidence-building interlude? Might he be the answer she sought?

Marriage to a marquis—that would be quite in keeping with the doings of a fairy godmother. For it would take a fairy godmother to bring it about. It seemed she would have to give serious consideration to such an arrangement.

They declared point, sequence and sets, and the game began. As Rushmere took the first trick, he directed at her that dazzling smile that would have sent one or two of her pupils—such as Miss Hanna Brookstone or Miss Sophronia Farhnam—off into a swoon of ecstasy. "Why can I not recall where we have met before, Miss—?" He broke off, inviting her to provide her name.

"Caldicot," she said. If he were not a gift of Xanthe's to her, the next information would cool the gleam in his eyes. "Until very recently, I was one of the instructresses at your daughter's school."

The gleam, if anything, brightened. "And what brings you to town? Or need I ask? The Saunderton child, I suppose. How very wise of her brother to keep so sharp an eye on her."

Phoebe stiffened. "Whatever can you mean, my lord?"

His eyebrows rose. "You need not pretend, you know. Her little escapades in Bath did not go unnoticed. I cannot blame Saunderton in the least for trying to marry her off as quickly as possible. But if I were you, I would keep my eye on that rather handsome lieutenant she was speaking with earlier."

She straightened, and fixed him with the quelling regard that sobered the more riotous of her former pupils. On him, it seemed to have no effect, but she pressed on anyway. "I am not here because of Miss Saunderton. Nor has she behaved in a manner that is in the least discreditable. A chance encounter has given rise to dreadful rumors, it is true, but I can assure you there is not one word of truth in them."

His eyebrows rose. "You would know best, of course."

"I do." She played her next card, then turned the conversation to the upcoming Season with more determination than finesse.

Over the next two hands, the unpleasantness faded to the back of her mind as they discussed the balls, plays, and other anticipated events of the upcoming weeks. He could be every bit as charming as her pupils claimed, she reflected when at last she rose. He came to his feet as well, claiming her hand as he thanked her for the games. His gaze holding hers, he carried her fingers to his lips. She inclined her head, accepting this gallantry as the flirtatious gesture it undoubtedly was, and they parted company.

Almost, she could regret the fact she would not be returning to the Misses Crippenham's establishment. But then Lady Jane Hatchard and Miss Georgeana Middleton would refuse to believe what had just occurred. She must remember to thank Xanthe for allowing this daydream to come true. Unless it was to be more than that. . . .

Musing on this, she strolled into the drawing room, where she saw Sir Miles Saunderton almost at once. That put her in mind of her reluctant promise to Lucilla, and, bracing herself, she strode up to him. He turned as she stopped at his side, and the frown lines lessened in his brow.

"You are looking grim," she said, which was not at all how she had meant to begin.

His lips twitched into a wry smile. "I had forgotten the difficulties of shepherding a green girl through a London Season."

She spotted Lucilla, who sat on one of the sofas beside a rather dashing Corinthian. His dress bespoke a sporting carelessness, and his handsome countenance betrayed a considerable amount of good humor. A marked familiarity showed in his manner, and she frowned. "Oh, dear, he seems just the sort of gentleman to most appeal to her. Is he dangerous?"

"Ashby? Lord, no." Sir Miles frowned. "Not to her, at least. If she only would take an interest in him, I would be glad. Unfortunately, they have known one another practically since she was in the cradle."

"A definite barrier to romance," Phoebe agreed, "but not insurmountable." She noticed Lucy's attention wander from one who should have been a most fascinating companion, her gaze drifting about the room until suddenly the girl's entire countenance lit with pleasure. Phoebe followed the direction of that gaze, and spotted her dashing lieutenant standing not far away, staring steadily back at Lucilla. Sir Miles, it seemed, had noticed the scarlet-coated officer, as well, and glowered at him. Curious, Phoebe asked, "Have you any objection to that lieutenant? He appears quite enamored of your sister."

"Enamored of her portion, you mean," Miles snapped. "I don't want any fortune hunter pursuing her."

"Are you positive that's what he is?"

He cast her an impatient glance. "Lucilla isn't the first heiress the fellow's made up to. And the devil's in it, she's too green to show any discretion."

Phoebe frowned. "It is a pity he is possessed of so pleasing a manner."

"A man bent on marrying an heiress can hardly be displeasing, can he?" came Miles's short answer.

With that, she had to agree.

"Ashby's popular enough with the other young ladies," he said in disgust. "He's forever having caps set for him."

But not the one he wanted? Did Lucy make the mistake of despising the familiar and being enchanted by the unknown? There sat Ashby, a matrimonial catch of no mean order, showering attentions upon the girl to the obvious envy of a number of other young ladies present. And Lucy remained oblivious to the singular honor he bestowed upon her.

"If he were to make another lady the object of his attentions, it might make her notice him," she said with diffidence.

He shot her a look from beneath his lowered brow. "Make her jealous, do you mean? But he'd never raise expectations he had no intention of fulfilling."

No, he wouldn't. Despite his modish dress, his sporting manner, he remained too obviously a man of honor. "If he were a touch less respectable, he would appeal more to a young girl with a romantic nature."

"Romantic!" Miles said the word with disgust. "How can any female turn her nose up at a matrimonial prize like Ashby in favor of some shady ne'er-do-well?"

"Simply because he is shady," Phoebe said, then gathered her courage to press on with her appointed task. "Sir Miles, if I might have a word with you in private?"

His gaze narrowed on her. "Difficult, in so crowded a party." He glanced about, then led the way to the apartment to which he had taken Lucy less than an hour before.

They left the door ajar, and Phoebe seated herself on a sofa at the far end of the room. "Please understand that I have no desire to interfere—"

"No," he murmured, "that would be meddling."

"You are not making this easy," she snapped. "I have only come to you because of my sincere attachment to Lucilla."

He inclined his head, but made no comment.

She rose, strode to the hearth while she searched for words, then turned to face him and plunged right in. "Sir Miles, I beg you will not forbid Lucilla to see her lieutenant."

His brow snapped down. "Do you desire me to permit her to throw herself away on a curst fortune hunter?"

"Do not be absurd. Only consider. She is of a romantic disposition. If you forbid what she believes to be her only chance for happiness, desperation will drive her into running away with him—or someone like him."

"So, I am to encourage her in her folly?"

"You can, if you insist, but I wouldn't recommend it. An attitude of amused tolerance will stand you in better stead."

"Amused tolerance is something I have grown rather good at," he admitted.

Her jaw tensed. "You may make jokes, of course," she said, "but I assure you, I have considerable experience with young ladies of her age and temperament. Please, for your sister's sake, consider what I have said." She hesitated a moment, then turned and left the room. Lucy, she feared, required a delicate touch to her bridle, while Sir Miles seemed to have a heavy hand where his sister was concerned. She could only hope her words had some effect on him.

The matter still occupied her mind when she emerged from the house the following morning, dressed in a rather stunning riding habit of emerald green velvet and a matching high-crowned hat with wisping veil. Really, it could be amazingly simple to turn oneself out in style if one only had a fairy godmother to lend a hand. As she started down the front steps, she suddenly realized that the skirt she lifted so she should not trip over it had changed to a ruby red. The next moment, the velvet became a rich sapphire blue, then a deep purple. Xanthe, apparently, still trying to make up her mind.

"I like green," she whispered. Her skirt flickered

through all the colors of the rainbow, then returned to the original emerald. "Thank you," Phoebe murmured, and turned her attention to the waiting Macha.

Another groom, holding three mounts, stood before the Saundertons' house. Phoebe would recognize that formidable roan anywhere, an admirable animal spoiling for a gallop. A chestnut stood solid at his side, ears back, but otherwise ignoring the antics of the sidling roan. So, too, did the third animal, a dainty, tranquil bay who stood with one back fetlock cocked, ears sideways, bordering on sleep. That could only be Lucilla's mount. The girl, as Phoebe well remembered from their brief excursions at the Misses Crippenham's Academy, did not enjoy equestrian activities. It surprised her that Lucy had consented to join this expedition—or that Sir Miles had consented to have her.

In any event, Sir Miles would not be pleased to see Phoebe mounting up, as well. She had best depart as quickly as possible. She turned to the groom, saying, "Good morning, Limmer," then bestowed the bits of the carrot she carried on both horses. Macha shoved gently against her, then lipped at her hand for more.

"Ready, miss?" Limmer moved to her side, preparing to toss her into the saddle.

The door of the neighboring house opened, and Lucy emerged onto the porch, yawning. "The day cannot possibly start this early," she protested, and cast an accusing glance into the sky, as if defying it to be light already.

"It is well advanced." Sir Miles, very much awake, followed his sister. "I did warn you last night when you said you wished to ride with me." He looked up, straight at Phoebe, and a slight frown flickered across his features. "Miss Caldicot, I see we are of the same mind. Would you care for company?"

For a brief moment she considered refusing, but that would be an unpardonable slight. Lucy chimed in, endorsing her brother's invitation, and Phoebe had no choice but to acquiesce with as much appearance of pleasure as she could muster. He had, after all, bestowed an amazingly amiable greeting upon her, considering what had passed between them the previous night.

He descended the shallow stairs, then strode over to join her, the controlled power of his step betraying his repressed energy. She realized her gaze lingered on him, and in embarrassment she turned away, back to her horse. Then he reached her side, and taking her hand, he bowed over it. No smile—but no open animosity, either. A truce, perhaps?

"Shall we be off? Your mare seems to be eager for her exercise." He cupped his hands, tossed her into the saddle, then gave more considerable help to his sister. In a very few minutes, he, too, swung himself onto his mount and turned the roan's head toward the park.

Lucy, fighting back another yawn, maneuvered her bay into position beside Phoebe. Macha tugged at the reins, striving to forge ahead, but Lucy's presence compelled Phoebe to restrain the eager mare to match the gelding's plodding pace. Sir Miles, not unexpectedly, moved ahead, his roan capering sideways, playing off his tricks.

Phoebe couldn't blame him for taking his moment

of freedom. She only wished she could do the same.
As it was, she could do no more than watch and admire the ease with which he sat his capricious mount's
tricks, the steadiness of his hands, the deep richness
of his chuckle as he brought the roan under control.

Lucilla sighed. "One must admit Miles is a capital
horseman."

"He is indeed." And what had passed between these
two since last Phoebe saw them? Then, they had barely
been on speaking terms with one another. Today, the
girl actually complimented her brother. *Had* Sir Miles
listened—and taken to heart—the unsolicited advice
she had thrust down his unwilling throat?

Lucy cast her a sideways glance. "I only got up this
morning so I would have the opportunity to thank you
for speaking to him. I am ever so grateful. Would you
believe it? He actually apologized to me."

"He—" Phoebe blinked. "No, I don't think I can
believe it."

Lucy laughed. "Now you are being absurd. Really,
Miles can be the best of good brothers. Most of the
time, that is. But he does so like to have everything—
and everyone—do just as he would wish. It can be so
very trying, at times, for he only sees things from his
own point of view."

"Which can prove difficult when it does not coin-
cide with yours," Phoebe agreed.

"Oh, you understand! But I knew you must, for you
have always been the dearest and best of my teachers.
You see, he doesn't believe in permitting love or—or
romance to interfere when he chooses our marriage
partners."

"He chooses?" That bald statement startled Phoebe.

"Only consider poor Amelia. She is next oldest after Miles, and had so many handsome beaus when she came to town, but Miles married her off to the dullest man who is quite elderly. Why, he must be five-and-forty if he is a day!"

"Must he?" Phoebe found herself floundering. "Perhaps she cared for him?"

"How could she? Only he is in the government, you must know, and will be given a title for his services, so Miles thought him an excellent match. And I dare say he never so much as consulted with Amelia about it."

Phoebe cut to the chase. "And is she dreadfully unhappy?"

Lucy considered, frowning. "Well, as to that, she seems content enough. Amelia was always the serious one. But how could she possibly prefer Mr. Brompton over her other suitors? And some of them were so very dashing! Pray do not say it is because Brompton is excessively rich, for I cannot believe Amelia to be so—so mercenary. No. Miles must have forced it upon her."

"I see. Poor Amelia. It must have been dreadful, with her crying throughout the wedding."

"Oh, but she didn't do that!" Lucy assured her quickly. "At least not that I ever heard. It all happened nearly eleven years ago, you must know, so I don't really remember any of it." She fell into a brooding silence.

Phoebe allowed it to continue until it seemed safe

to change the subject. "Do you attend the Reardons' ball next week?"

Her attempt to divert Lucy's mind failed. "Harry had more spirit," the girl said suddenly, "but even he did as Miles bid, in the end. He was the next eldest, after Amelia, you must know, but he was killed at Salamanca. He'd married an heiress the year before, and Miles must have arranged it, for she was quite fubsy-faced, and they had known one another since they were in their infancy, for her estate bordered ours, and Miles always said how suitable such a match would be."

"I thought Lord Ashby's—" Phoebe began.

"The *other* side," Lucy explained, as if to a dullard.

"Of course, how silly of me. But perhaps there had been an attachment of long-standing between Harry and his bride," Phoebe suggested.

Lucy wrinkled her nose. "I told you, they grew up like brother and sister, just like Ashby and I have. One cannot possibly fall in love under such circumstances." She waved a dismissive hand. "Then there is Juliana. She agreed to the marriage Miles arranged for her, but only because the Earl of Falmouth offered for Miss Hartley rather than her and she was so very chagrined. But she has quite reconciled herself to it, since her husband is a leader of society, and she so very much enjoys being a notable society hostess. She would have brought me out, but of course you know all that. And of course Susanna—she is my next sister, and only three years older than I am—she never wished to marry at all, but Miles insisted, and so she accepted a naval captain who is away for years upon end, and so she has both her independence and the protection of being married, though she cannot be in love."

"I see." This family portrait fascinated Phoebe. And always Miles managing the affairs of his siblings. "Your father died when you were quite young?" she hazarded.

"Oh, when I was still in leading strings. He and Mama both together, in a carriage accident. I always thought how very romantic that must be, to die in the arms of the man you love."

Dying in a carriage accident didn't sound the least bit romantic to Phoebe, but she held her tongue. Sir Miles Saunderton might be autocratic, but it began to sound to Phoebe as if there might be some cause. It could not be easy inheriting the responsibility of a large and hopeful family at what must have been a very young age. He could not have been any older than Lucilla, if that much.

Her companion cast her a sideways glance. "No one ever believes how managing Miles truly is. You see, he can be so very affable—the best of brothers, in fact—when the matter is trivial. But when one's heart is involved, he can turn into the greatest beast in nature."

"But not out of any sense of malice," Phoebe pointed out

Lucy frowned. "No," she agreed at last. "Out of a sense that he knows better than you. He just doesn't understand!"

On this plaintive note, they reached the park. Sir Miles had already entered the gate and now walked his roan in circles, waiting for them to join him. Lucy hung back, and Phoebe, with an apology made unnecessary by the curvets of her mare, left the girl to the care of the grooms.

"I fear you had a slow time of it," Sir Miles said as she joined him.

"It was a pleasure." She brought Macha abreast of him, and the two horses quickened their pace.

He shot her a penetrating glance. "Perhaps I can make it up to you with a gallop? Lucy will be all right with the grooms."

"A delightful idea." Phoebe loosened her rein, and her mount broke into a controlled canter. Sir Miles kept pace, and Phoebe allowed Macha her head. They raced forward, with the great roan half a nose in the lead. They might have continued indefinitely had they not come upon a gentleman and two grooms, obviously engaged in the early stages of introducing a set of young and flighty animals to the park. Sir Miles reined in a second before Phoebe, and they slowed to a prancing walk long before they would pose a threat to the other riders.

"Cuthbert isn't finished," Sir Miles said, patting the roan's neck that bore only the faintest flecks of sweat.

"We could race back," Phoebe suggested.

"I would rather have a chance to speak with you." He turned the discontented Cuthbert around.

Phoebe followed suit, aware of a sudden unease. But whether it came from herself, or from him, she couldn't be certain. She remained silent, waiting for him to continue.

"Perhaps Lucilla has already confided in you that

I took your advice." He spoke the words stiffly, as if such an admission came only with difficulty to him.

"I should thank you for not ignoring it simply because it came from me."

That brought a smile to his lips. "I acknowledged your experience in dealing with romantic young ladies." He rode in silence for a long minute, then added, "I only hope I have done the right thing."

"I gathered your other sisters were of a more practical turn of mind."

"Lord, yes. Did Lucy tell you that? I thought her bent on turning them all into tragic heroines, doomed to loveless marriages by my machinations."

He said this with such a wry tone that it forced Phoebe to laugh. "Something like that," she admitted.

"Lucy will tell you I haven't a romantic bone in my body, and it is probably true."

It dawned on Phoebe she was beginning to have trouble remembering how very angry she was with him. He had, in fact, a disturbing ability to disarm her. She found that unsettling. The last thing she needed in her life was a meddling, managing gentleman who had already caused her a great deal of trouble.

Ahead of them, Phoebe caught sight of Lucy. But the girl no longer rode under the escort of Limmer and the Saundertons' groom. Those two had dropped behind, allowing her to ride at the side of a gentleman whose scarlet coat proclaimed him to be an officer. And not just any officer, Phoebe wagered. Somehow, Lieutenant Gregory Harwich had joined Lucy.

She felt the force of Miles's glare even before she turned to look at him.

He sat rigid at her side, his glower fixed on her rather than his sister. "I hope, Miss Caldicot," he said through clenched teeth, "I will not have cause to regret *your* meddling."

Six

Over the course of the next few days, Miles saw very little of Miss Caldicot. Twice she appeared in time to join him for his morning ride, but she remained aloof, as if only the politeness due to a neighbor kept her from refusing his escort. She did not display any of that reticence when she spoke to other gentlemen, though. Only the other night he'd glimpsed her taking part in a country dance at an informal hop with Viscount Wolverhampton, and they had seemed to be upon excellent terms.

Nor did she drive alone in the park during the hour of the Promenade. Once he'd seen her up beside his good friend, the elegant Mr. Charles Dauntry, and another time her escort had been none other than the Marquis of Rushmere. The lady, it seemed, did not lack for eligible suitors.

Lucy thought it a rare joke that the leaders of society flocked to pay homage to her erstwhile deportment mistress. She even went so far as to write a letter to her dear friend Miss Hanna Brookstone, still incarcerated at the Misses Crippenham's Academy, informing her of their dear Miss Caldicot's stunning success, with particular reference to Rushmere. This resulted, less than a week later, in Miss Brookstone's eruption upon the town in the tow of a matchmaking mama of formidable experience and determination.

Lucy greeted the arrival of Miss Brookstone with delight, and bore her next door upon a morning visit to their former instructress. There, as they later informed Miles in awed accents, they had encountered Rushmere himself, along with Viscount Wolverhampton. There could be not a doubt of it, they exclaimed; Miss Caldicot was destined to contract a brilliant alliance. Miles could only hope Lucy would succumb to a determination to emulate her, and abandon her passion for uniforms.

It pleased him, for some obscure reason, when he emerged from the house two mornings later with a yawning Lucy at his side to find Miss Caldicot seated atop her mare, adjusting the folds of her voluminous skirts. The emerald of her habit suited her, the thought flashed through his mind. She greeted Lucy with her usual warmth; he himself, though, earned no more than the coolest of good mornings.

She accepted their escort as far as the park, but once within its gates, she moved ahead to meet a gentleman on a lanky chestnut. Charles Dauntry, Miles noted with disapproval, then wondered at such negative feelings for one he considered a good friend. Perhaps it had something to do with the fact that although they remained a foursome, Miss Caldicot chose to ride at Charles's side, leaving Miles to bring up the rear with Lucy.

When at last they returned to Half Moon Street—

free of Mr. Dauntry's company—it occurred to Miles that everything seemed oddly quiet, considering that Lady Xanthe would give a musical *soiree* that evening. None of the usual signs of activity engulfed her abode. Miles regarded it with the perplexity of a gentleman whose own home frequently had been thrown into chaotic disorder while the designated hostess ruthlessly prepared for an invasion by society's elite. Miss Caldicot, he noted, eyed the tranquil scene with complete unconcern.

"Where are the tradesmen?" cried Lucilla, who had been riding in silence beside Miss Caldicot. "Ought there not to be an army of them bustling down your area steps right about now? There always is every time we entertain, and starting with first dawn," she added with feeling.

"Is there?" Miss Caldicot looked from one to the other of them, her expression arrested. "But then it is only a small party, after all."

A sudden smile tugged at the corner of Miles's mouth. "The size of the gathering rarely seems to matter," he explained.

"Oh." She considered a moment. "Well, you might as well enjoy the quiet while you can, then. I feel certain the storm of activity shall break at any moment." She jumped lightly from her saddle before Miles could move to help her, bid them both a good morning, thanked Limmer as she handed over the mare, and hurried up the stairs.

Miles swung to the ground, then lifted his sister to the paving at his side. "She seems remarkably calm for her first party," Miles said.

Lucilla waved it aside. "She is always calm. It is a great pity you cannot like her better. Indeed, she is the best of good—" She broke off as a rumbling of wheels started, and one after another, half a dozen carts and wagons trundled around the corner and down the street toward them. "There," Lucy pronounced. "All the tradesmen you could wish."

As the entourage pulled up before them, several windows of Lady Xanthe's house flew wide, and servants appeared, aproned footmen shaking small carpets, mobcapped maids discharging the contents of their dusters. Two more footmen emerged from the front door, polishing buckets and cloths in hand. Miles and Lucy beat a hasty retreat into the sanctuary of their own home.

The chaos next door continued throughout the morning. Miles sought refuge at his club, and was relieved to discover, when he returned at last, that calm had once again reasserted itself. This left him free to dress for dinner, to which Lady Xanthe had invited his family, in peace. In honor of the occasion, he astounded his man Vines by requesting, in the most casual voice possible, his late father's heavy fob and the emerald stick pin for his neckcloth. Armed with both of these, he descended to the salon to find, for once, both his Aunt Jane and Lucy there before him.

Aunt Jane looked up from her glass of negus, and her eyes twinkled. "Very elegant, Miles."

Lucy, who had been peering into the gilt-framed mirror over the hearth, spun about, then ran to throw her arms about him, exclaiming, "Thank you, *dearest* of brothers."

"Do you want to ruin my neckcloth?" he demanded, disentangling her with care.

"Not for worlds! Oh, Miles, you *do* like Miss Caldicot. I was so afraid— But that is neither here nor there. She is the greatest dear, is she not? And so very lovely."

"A veritable rose," came Miles's prompt response. "Complete with very long and very sharp thorns."

Lucy fell back a step. "But I thought—I hoped—"

"A waste of time, my dear." He had *not* donned the fob and pin for Miss Caldicot's sake. It had merely pleased him to wear them this night. Whether that young woman liked them or not was a matter of complete indifference to him.

Lucy sighed. "At least you will refrain from arguing with her?"

He raised his eyebrows. "When I am a guest in her home? Thank you, but I should hope I would not be guilty of such a want of conduct. Shall we go?"

A few minutes later, Lady Xanthe's majordomo opened the door to them, relieved them of their wraps, and ushered them across the entry hall. To the accompaniment of his ringing voice announcing their names, they entered a spacious salon decorated in tones of muted green, ivory and gold. Fresh flowers clustered in bowls on every surface, giving the impression of a garden.

He greeted his hostess, then turned to her protege. For a moment he simply stared; then he recollected himself and stepped forward to greet her. It took an effort, though, to keep his expression bland. The pale-blue crepe of her flounced gown set lights dancing in

her misty eyes, while the filmy white of the under-
gown, which ended in a single flounce, provided just
the right touch of elegance to one of her slight build.
He didn't normally pay much heed to feminine fashion
and furbelows, but he could recognize a perfect effect
when he saw one.

She'd finished herself off with the right touch, too.
A strand of creamy pearls hung about her throat, a
small grouping of pearls clustered at each ear, and she
had arranged her copious amounts of coppery brown
hair in vastly becoming curls. As he drew closer, he
detected the delicate scent of violets that clung to her.
The result went to his head like a fine brandy.

She took his hand with aloof detachment. "As you
see," she said, her voice as cool as a shady stream,
"we have been quite as busy as you could wish."

"You have, indeed. You are to be congratulated."

Her brow creased, and a faint color tinged her
cheeks. "I did not seek a compliment."

No, she wouldn't. Not from him, at least. She made
that clear enough. He inclined his head, but before he
could speak again, Lucy swept toward them.

She clasped her former instructress's hands. "Oh,
Miss Caldicot, I have never seen you look so lovely.
Is she not beautiful, Miles?"

"You must not place your brother in so awkward a
position," Miss Caldicot responded before Miles could
speak. She then led his sister off to discuss the merits
of the ball gown Lucy had ordered that afternoon.

Dinner passed with surprising ease, mostly because
he and Miss Caldicot exchanged only the merest com-
monplaces. They finished barely minutes before the

first carriage pulled up in the street, and his hostesses made their way to the top of the stairs to greet their arriving guests. Miles escorted his aunt and sister to the elegant drawing room where a large harp, a pianoforte, and a cello held positions of prominence.

A cello. Miles strolled forward to examine the instrument, running his fingers along the gleaming wood. He hadn't played in months. He touched the strings, and a haunting tune filled his mind, a humming that wrapped its melodic threads through him. He took the chair, rosined the bow with an abstracted frown, checked to find the instrument perfectly in tune, then sought the chords and notes that would reproduce that remarkable song.

He held the final tone, drawing it out until it at last fell silent. For a long moment he sat wrapped in his music, until an odd, discordant noise smote his ears. He opened eyes he hadn't realized he'd closed, and saw perhaps a score of people sitting about the room, applauding. He hadn't meant to play for anyone's entertainment but his own. He stood, laying the instrument aside, bowed, and retreated to the back wall of the room.

"That was wonderful," a soft voice said at his side. "I had no idea you played."

He looked down to see Miss Caldicot, her eyes glowing, an odd, searching expression in their depths. It caught at him, holding him immobile, wiping every conscious thought from his mind. He saw only her beautiful mist-colored eyes, felt only the responding tug of a bond forging between them. Awareness filled him, of her scent, of her tentative smile, of *her.*

And then she was gone, slipping away to greet more new arrivals, and the spell broke. The impulse lingered to follow her, to speak to her, but now, with so many people about, did not seem the time. Nor did he know precisely what he wished to say. Instead, he leaned against the wall and listened to the elderly Lord Grantley, who had brought a violin and a pronounced taste for ballads, and convinced himself his imagination ran riot where Miss Caldicot was concerned.

Yet, as if of its own volition, his gaze strayed back to her. She sat on the far side of the room—and not alone, naturally. The tall, arrogant figure of the Marquis of Rushmere occupied the place at her side. His head bent toward her, and he spoke words that seemed intended for her ears alone.

The damned man flirted with her. Anger welled within Miles, surprising by its very existence. Why the devil should it matter to him whom Miss Caldicot encouraged? Yet infuriatingly, it did. He considered the matter and decided it was because the marquis was an unprincipled rake, and he didn't want to see someone of whom his sister was fond taken in by a man who would think nothing of ruining her. He had shepherded too many sisters through this particular forest of wolves not to recognize the need to take action.

What he would do, precisely, would depend on Rushmere. Miles would have to give the matter some thought. Miss Caldicot was not a young lady who would take kindly to his meddling in her affairs. But he had no intention of letting that stop him.

Two middle-aged gentlemen—Mr. Colney with his oboe, and Sir Roderick Leyland with the cello—struck up a duet with the ease of long practice. Out of the corner of his eye, he saw Miss Caldicot wave to someone, and the next moment Charles Dauntry strolled over to join her. That ought to please him more than it did.

As the music drew to a close, Lady Xanthe called for an interval, and Dauntry led Miss Caldicot off to find refreshment. Mr. Colney, Miles noted with amusement, tucked away his oboe and turned to Aunt Jane, greeting her with all the warmth of an old friendship. He wouldn't have to worry about her entertainment for a little while. Which left only Lucy.

He spotted her sitting with Miss Hanna Brookstone and Simon Ashby. Or perhaps it was more accurate to say that Miss Brookstone sat with Lord Ashby, and Lucy merely happened to share the same sofa with her two friends. Ashby had been speaking, and Miss Brookstone hung upon his every word. Lucy, oblivious to both appearances and their conversation, kept skewing about, peering at the door, then at the mantel clock, her expression both earnest and impatient. Disappointment awaited her, Miles reflected, if she hoped to see Lieutenant Harwich this night. He could think of no gentleman less likely for Lady Xanthe to invite to her party.

Ashby excused himself and strode over to speak with Sir Roderick Leyland. Hanna Brookstone at once grasped Lucy's hands, compelling the other girl's attention, and launched into some whispered confidence. She really was a pretty chit, Miles reflected, watching her animated countenance. She possessed a plump softness set off by ringlets the color of ripe corn and a gown of pink gauze that matched the roses in her cheeks. Her manners were all one could wish for in a well-bred young lady, but she possessed a silliness he could only be grateful Lucy didn't share. She would probably make an excellent match.

Lucy straightened and stared at her friend, frowning. Miss Brookstone giggled and nodded, but Lucy only scowled all the more. She made some short answer that drew an indignant exclamation from Miss Brookstone and sent her off in a flounce. Curious, Miles joined his sister.

Lucy looked up at him, her expression vexed. "Hanna is in raptures over Simon," she informed him.

"So are a number of other young ladies," he reminded her.

She waved that aside. "Oh, he can be quite engaging when he puts his mind to it, I suppose. But the way she looked up at him, fluttering her eyelashes and flirting in the most outrageous manner! I would never do anything so vulgar." She cast a darkling glance across the room to where Ashby remained with Sir Roderick. "And he was just as bad." She sniffed. "I daresay he likes obvious females."

Miles could not help but be pleased. It would do Lucy a great deal of good to see her old friend through the eyes of another young lady. It just might make her forget scarlet coats.

People milled back into the room, and groups shifted while everyone found new seats. Lady Xanthe drew Miss Caldicot toward the pianoforte, and Miles's interest roused. He moved to the wall, where he stood with his shoulder propped against it and his arms folded, and watched as she settled at the instrument, hesitated a moment, then began on a ballad of treacherous love.

Her voice suited her, he decided, delicate yet clear, intense and haunting. He could listen to her for a very long time. Yet the song ended all too soon, and she left the instrument. The buzz of conversation, which had stilled for her performance, broke out again as Charles Dauntry moved to intercept her. She evaded him with an apologetic smile, responding instead to an imperious summons by his Aunt Jane. Miles strolled over to join them.

As he approached, Miss Caldicot looked up, met his gaze, and soft color tinged her cheeks. She looked away.

"I am glad to see that years of instructing less than talented young ladies has not destroyed your love of music," he said.

At that, an impish smile flickered in her eyes. "How do you know it has not?"

"No one could play and sing as you do if it had," he said simply.

Her color deepened. "You flatter me, sir."

He shook his head. "If you are brave, perhaps we might try a duet at some time."

She met his gaze, and her smile faded. Somewhere behind them a violinist and flautist tuned briefly, then launched into a lively piece by Mozart. Miles found that for once he had found something—or rather someone—of more interest than the music. He stared into her eyes, which reflected the sparkle of the candles, the sparkle of her lively spirit. An impulse, almost overpowering, seized him, to run his fingers through her silken curls.

"Why not try a piece together some night soon?" Aunt Jane suggested. Miles stiffened. He had forgotten her presence. For that matter, he'd forgotten everyone else in the room, as well. A damned fool he must look, gazing like a moonling at a lovely face. "An excellent suggestion," he said, inserting a casual note into his voice. "If you and Lady Xanthe could join us for dinner, we could try our hands at a piece or two."

Phoebe returned a tentative answer and moved away to consult her godmother about a possible date. Miles turned back to the musicians, until a young lady took up her place at the harp, an instrument he cordially detested. He could easily slip out in search of refreshments for a few minutes. He reached the door, only to fall back a pace as a slight gentleman in scarlet regimentals hurried up the steps from the ground floor. Lieutenant Gregory Harwich made an elegant leg to him, flashed him the brilliant smile that so affected foolishly romantic young ladies like Lucilla, and swept past him into the drawing room.

Lucilla sprang to her feet, causing her neighbors to turn to stare at her, then stood, hands clasped, her heart blatant in her expression, as her officer made his way to her side. He seized both her hands, carried them to his lips, then sank to the sofa at her side, drawing her down with him. Not a single word passed between them, but there was no need. Their besotted gazes spoke far too eloquently.

Miss Caldicot, interfering again, Miles fumed. He could think of no other explanation for that damned fellow to be here. He started forward, to drag Lucy away by any means necessary, only to catch sight of Miss Caldicot hurrying toward him. He didn't stop.

Her hand caught his arm. "Please, Sir Miles."

He spun to face her, glaring. "What the devil do you mean, inviting that man here?" he hissed in a voice that took every ounce of his willpower to keep low.

She pulled on his arm, coaxing him from the room. "You must not create a scene," she whispered. "And smile at me, for heaven's sake, or you will cause the very scandal you hope to avoid." With an obvious effort, she forced the corners of her mouth upward.

He did the same, though doubted he fooled anyone. With at least the appearance of complacence, he allowed her to draw him from the apartment and down the hall to the dining room. "I should have thought this was one house where my sister would be safe from his machinations. Do you enjoy watching my sister make a spectacle of herself over a blatant fortune hunter?"

"It is no such thing, and so you would realize if you didn't let your temper override your judgment. How can she possibly come to know him if she is never permitted to see him?"

"My point, exactly," he snapped.

"Would you rather your sister be permitted to build dreams about him, turn him into a hero in her heart? It is better by far for her to come to know the real man."

He glowered at her. "That's not something she is likely to do. The fellow is an expert at engaging the affections of young ladies, at disguising his own mercenary motives. The result will be that the foolish girl will fancy herself in love with him, and then there'll be the devil to pay, and no pitch hot."

"How can you know he is truly so terrible if you do not come to know him, yourself?" Phoebe demanded. "You know nothing of him."

"I know he is not a member of Whites, nor of Brooks. I know that he has never been inside Almack's, and that he has dangled after at least three heiresses during the last year, two of them daughters of cits. Is that not sufficient? Yet here you are, interfering with my efforts to see my sister safely married to a gentleman of sense and respectability."

"Lucilla doesn't want sense and respectability," Phoebe informed him. "She wants romance. And if you thought about it for a moment, you'd see you're providing her with that romance by making her think herself a tragic heroine. Believe me, opposition is fatal."

His jaw clenched. "You may be an expert in the schoolroom, Miss Caldicot, but allow me to be a better judge of the world. I will be grateful to you if you will refrain from meddling in my sister's affairs."

She flushed, and anger flashed in her eyes. "Someone has to interfere with your outrageous managing. Lucilla regards Lord Ashby as a friend and cannot imagine marrying him—at the moment."

"So you believe I should permit her to throw herself away on an unprincipled fortune hunter?"

"I believe nothing of the sort!" she snapped back. "But tonight she has felt the first stirrings of jealousy over Lord Ashby. And if I know Hanna Brookstone, there will be many more to come. Give them a chance to develop, and she'll lose interest in so easy a conquest as her lieutenant."

"Or she'll run off with him," he countered.

"Only if you raise so much opposition that she feels it to be her only choice."

He regarded her in exasperation. "Do you enjoy trying to manage everyone's affairs, or merely my sister's?"

Her color darkened. "I don't know why I waste my time talking to you. If I hadn't promised Lucy—" She broke off. Without another word, she strode from the room.

So Lucy had begged her to intervene. He should have guessed.

He did not, as temper urged him, leave the party; that would be to allow Lucilla free rein in her folly. Instead, he joined his sister and Lieutenant Harwich and forced himself to be polite to the man. He found it a strain, but the surprised and gratified glances directed at him by Lucy made the effort worthwhile. The irritating suspicion that Miss Caldicot might, perhaps, be right upon this one point galled him.

He didn't speak to Miss Caldicot again that night except to take his leave. In the morning, somewhat to his surprised annoyance, she did not emerge from her house to indulge in an early ride. He took his exercise alone, and found this normally enjoyable pastime did little to ease his growing temper. He returned early, only to pace restlessly about the house until his aunt objected that she would never know a moment's peace as long as he remained indoors. Miles took the hint and departed for his club.

By the time he had enjoyed a few hands of piquet with Charles Dauntry, visited his tailor, ordered a new pair of riding boots, and talked Wolverhampton out of purchasing an overly ornate snuff box, it was time to change into riding dress and join the fashionable Promenade through Hyde Park. He found his aunt on her bed recruiting her energies for the evening's jollifications, and his sister already departed in the company of Lady Xanthe, Miss Caldicot, and Hanna Brookstone. Miles sent for Cuthbert and set off in pursuit of the ladies.

They were surprisingly easy to find, though not easy to reach. Lady Xanthe's barouche stood to the side of the carriage drive about halfway around the circuit, surrounded by a horde of gentlemen on horseback, who resolved themselves into Simon Ashby, Charles Dauntry, Viscount Wolverhampton, and the Marquis of Rushmere. Miles urged Cuthbert forward and worked his way into the throng.

"Miles!" Lucy waved gaily at him as he maneuvered into position between the marquis and Dauntry. "Rushmere has just suggested the most wonderful scheme. We are all to be his guests for a tour of Hampton Court!"

Miles turned to the marquis, who sat astride a large, lanky black with a flashy blaze and stocking. "And when is this expedition to be?"

"Three days hence—if that is convenient?" He spoke to them all, but his gaze rested on Miss Caldicot, making it abundantly clear for whose pleasure he had planned this party.

It was Lady Xanthe who answered. "It is very kind of you, to be sure, but I quite regret that Mrs. Mannering and I have other plans."

Lucilla turned to her, her face a picture of dismay. "Aunt Jane cannot go? Oh, that is too dreadful. It would have been the most delightful of treats."

"There is no need to fret, my dear." Xanthe bestowed a smile on her. "I daresay there need not be the least objection to your brother acting as your escort. And if you are both to go, then I need not scruple to permit Phoebe to make one of the party."

Lucy brightened and turned toward him. "Oh, pray say we may go, Miles."

"Yes." Rushmere awarded him a civil smile. "Do say you will come."

Miles experienced an overwhelming temptation to claim a prior engagement, simply to scotch the man's plans. But if he did, the marquis might well find another way to spend the day in Miss Caldicot's company, which Miles felt was an occurrence to be prevented. He forced a smile and said, "I shall look forward to it," and did an admirable job of keeping his sarcasm from sounding in his voice.

"Excellent." Rushmere eyed the group. "Miss Caldicot, will you do me the honor of riding with me in my curricle?"

A delicate flush tinged Miss Caldicot's cheeks. Very becomingly, at that. What right had Rushmere to make her blush with pleasure? But as long as that unprincipled rake gave her no other cause, he would be satisfied.

"Thank you," she said simply.

The marquis beamed at her. "Then, I shall call for you on Thursday at nine in the morning. If you will excuse me? I have more invitations to extend." He swept off his hat in farewell, but his smiling gaze lingered on Miss Caldicot a moment before he wheeled his horse and rode off.

The situation might be worse, Miles reflected as the barouche maneuvered once more into the line of traffic. Ashby, Dauntry and Wolverhampton trailed after it, with Miles remaining close to the carriage. At least Lieutenant Gregory Harwich was not likely to make up one of the party. That meant for once he could relax his vigil on Lucy—and direct it instead toward protecting Miss Caldicot.

That young lady said something which he didn't quite hear, but Lucy, who sat at her side, laughed gaily. "It is *you* who has been singled out for this honor. Do you honestly believe for a moment he would have invited any of the rest of us had we not been in your company?"

Which was exactly what Miles was thinking, but he didn't like the idea any better when his sister voiced it.

"Oh, if only the other girls at school could see this," giggled Hanna Brookstone. "He is their idol, dear Lady Xanthe, yet it is our own Miss Caldicot he seeks out."

"They would refuse to believe it," said Lucy.

Miss Caldicot directed a quelling glance first at

Lucy, then at Hanna. "I, too, refuse to believe it, so let us have no more of this nonsense, please."

"But he is quite one of the most sought after gentlemen in London," cried Hanna. "And since the death of his wife, he has had uncounted caps set for him. Oh, Miss Caldicot, just think if he should offer for you! That would be such a triumph, for he is quite the greatest matrimonial prize imaginable, not to mention being such a dashing, romantic gentleman." The girl blinked at her former instructress. "You do not look pleased."

Miss Caldicot cast an odd glance at her godmother. "It seems such a very unlikely thing for him to do, does it not?"

Lady Xanthe returned the regard with unusual solemnity. "Should you like it?"

Lucy laughed. "Of course she would. Why, any lady would be in alt at the mere prospect!"

Miss Caldicot shook her head. "This is all the most complete nonsense. He is merely indulging in a flirtation, probably being kind because I am one of his daughter's instructresses. He doesn't mean anything by it. I would be foolish beyond permission if I were to refine upon his attentions."

And that, Miles reflected, was the most sensible speech he had ever heard made by a marriageable young lady. Now, if only he could convince himself she meant it.

Xanthe knelt in the corner of her room, rummaging through the collection of beeswax tapers that lay in the ashwood box on the floor. She hesitated over her choice, then drew out three of the candles, one of pink for love, one of light blue to open understanding, and one of white to ward away doubts and fears. Humming softly, she arranged them in holders on the lace cloth.

A curious *myap* sound came from the bed where Titus lay with his tail wrapped about his body, watching.

"Because she used a candle when she made her original wish," Xanthe told the feline. "Make yourself useful and come breathe on the flames."

The cat unwound himself, stretched luxuriously, then sprang lightly from the coverlet, sauntered across the room, and in one leap landed before the tapers she arranged in a triangle. He sniffed each one, then looked at her expectantly.

"She's very difficult," Xanthe told Titus, who merely flicked an ear in response. She regarded him with a touch of exasperation. "Well, what would you call someone who cannot see the obvious? She looks for her answer everywhere except in the right place."

Titus made a derisive sound.

She shook her head. "Coming right out and simply telling someone their answer never works. You know that. She has to find it out for herself."

The very tip of Titus's tail twitched, and he emitted a silent meow.

Xanthe's mischievous smile flashed. "Don't be absurd. I'm not actually telling her anything. I doubt she'd listen, anyway. I'm just nudging things a little."

Titus didn't deign to reply. He merely sat back on his haunches, waiting.

"I just thought it might be helpful," she said, and her voice took on a defensive note, "if one or two people were to display their true natures."

Titus regarded her, unblinking.

Xanthe stared at the cat, but no further comments were forthcoming. Satisfied, she began to hum softly as she inscribed an ancient symbol directly in front of the candles, and all three burst into flame. The sweet scents of rose, cardamom, and lavender mingled in the air, and a trace of smoke rose from each taper, spiraling upward, intertwining in a mystic dance. Xanthe rubbed her hands together, her humming changed to a mysterious, lilting tune, and she got down to business.

Seven

The day of the expedition to Hampton Court dawned bright and clear, the deep blue of the sky accented by puffy white clouds. It still lacked a quarter of an hour before nine—the appointed time when Rushmere would drive his curricle to the door at Half Moon Street—but Phoebe waited, already gowned in a carriage dress of bottle green muslin.

She turned from her bedroom window and regarded her reflection once more in the cheval glass. "I think it looked better in that lighter shade," she said after a moment.

Xanthe, who had seated herself hovering four feet in the air—the better to see her protege from all angles, she had said, though Phoebe strongly suspected she did it merely for the fun of it—floated closer, then down to the same level as Phoebe. "I've been thinking—" She broke off and hummed a single bar, then said, "Look again. Do you not think the russet hue is vastly becoming?"

A meow sounded from the window, and Titus turned to regard them, the tip of his tail twitching.

"Your marquis," Xanthe informed her, "has just turned onto the street."

Phoebe, who had reached for her bonnet, stopped. She turned her serious regard on her godmother. "Is he? *My* marquis, I mean?"

Xanthe smiled that mysterious smile that gave nothing away. "Don't you know?"

Phoebe set the bonnet on her head and tied the ribands into a bow. "No," she said at last. "I don't."

"Well." Xanthe bestowed that aggravating smile on her once more. "You had best go down if you do not want to keep him waiting."

Why could Xanthe not give her a definite answer? Phoebe reflected as she descended the stairs to the hall. If one's fairy godmother presented one with a marquis, one would be foolish to whistle him down the wind. Yet despite Rushmere's attentiveness since her arrival in town, Phoebe could not be certain of the outcome of this wish of hers.

She had expected to fall head over heels in love, she supposed. Only she hadn't. She was flattered by his attentions, of course. She was vividly aware of the social and financial advantages of the union. Such a husband could ease Thomas's future in a manner that could not help but make a loving sister recognize her obvious duty. So today she would take a long look at Rushmere to discover in him why it was that Xanthe had produced him for her.

As she reached the foot of the stair, the knocker sounded on the door. She stepped quickly into the Ivory Salon, waiting for one of the servants to open to him. Her gown, she noted with a touch of amusement, had returned to the flattering pale green she had liked. Peeping out the window, she beheld not the sporting racing curricle she had expected, but a high-perch phaeton, a treacherous vehicle, and driven uni-corn, at that. Rushmere himself sat on the precarious seat, walking his team of three very flashy blacks. He had sent his groom to announce his arrival. That dis-turbed her—though he probably entrusted those re-markable cattle of his to no one. She returned to the hall, thanked Arthur, and accompanied the groom down the steps to await the return of the dashing equi-page.

The Saundertons' groom drove up, and Miles and Lucilla emerged from their house. Lucy greeted her with delight, hurrying over to join her. "It is going to be so much fun," she cried as she reached Phoebe. "Oh, my dear Miss Caldicot, I am so looking forward to this."

The mischievous twinkle in her eye did not escape Phoebe's notice. The girl had been up to something, but what it was, she couldn't tell. She determined to keep an eye on her, though what trouble even so en-terprising a young lady as Lucy could get into at Hampton Court while a member of a private party, and under her brother's chaperonage at that, she couldn't tell.

The phaeton appeared again, and Miles's eyebrows rose. "An unusual choice of vehicle," he said.

"What a mark of honor," Lucy cried. "He must be determined for you to have the greatest treat today." She sighed. "How much I wish some gentleman would make such romantic gestures for me."

"Romantic, perhaps," said Miles dryly. "But deucedly uncomfortable, I should imagine."

Rushmere drew abreast of them, then swung down from his precarious perch to assist Phoebe up to the seat. This proved no easy feat to accomplish, but Phoebe at last achieved her goal amid considerable laughter which she hoped hid a touch of embarrassment. Rushmere mounted with the ease of practice, setting the vehicle swaying in a manner that left Phoebe a touch queasy. Miles and Lucilla, she noted, already waited in their curricle.

Rushmere gave his horses the office, and Lucy, who had been scanning the street, called, "Are we not to wait for Simon?"

"Ashby is picking up Miss Brookstone," Rushmere told her. "They'll join us in the park."

"Simon is driving Hanna?" Lucy stiffened and turned to Miles. "I thought Mr. Dauntry would bring her."

"Ashby spoke up more quickly." Her brother waved the phaeton ahead.

"I thought Simon wished to ride beside us." A note of petulance crept into her voice.

The vehicles separated, making conversation between them impossible, and Phoebe cast an uncertain glance at the marquis, searching for an opening gambit. At last, she tried, "Miss Saunderton assures me that all my former pupils would be quite green with envy if they knew you had driven me in your famous carriage."

He spared a rapid glance from his mettlesome team,

and the smile he flashed her could only be described as seductive. "I am gratified that you are pleased."

What she really was, she reflected, was simply hanging on. It took every ounce of her concentration to keep her balance with any degree of credit as they jostled and bounced over the cobblestones. And there was Lucy, riding quite at her ease, she noted with a touch of envy. In fact, Sir Miles's carriage bore every appearance of being exceptionally well sprung, and his pair of gleaming bays looked to her to be sweet goers. Dash wasn't always what it was cracked up to be. Perhaps she should change vehicles with Lucy to give the girl some practical experience with that fact.

Once they had maneuvered themselves into the flow of wagons and carriages that filled the street, Rushmere relaxed his attention from the difficult task of controlling his trio, and addressed a flirtatious remark to Phoebe that brought warm color to her cheeks. Before long, he had set up a flow of teasing, lighthearted comments that were a trifle too warm for her taste. The uneasy suspicion crossed her mind that a gentleman would not speak in so free and easy a manner before the lady he desired to make his wife.

At last they pulled through the gates of the park, and with a sensation of relief she spotted Charles Dauntry on his rawboned gray trotting toward them. He reached the phaeton and swept his curly beaver from his head, his eyes smiling as he greeted her. But before Phoebe could do more than say "Good morning," Rushmere's leader skipped sideways, and with a curt word of excuse he set them cantering ahead, leaving Dauntry to join Miles and Lucy.

As they swept past the curricle, she saw that Lucy now drove the bays under her brother's expert guidance. "How kind of him," Phoebe exclaimed, pleased by this sign of sibling harmony. "She has been longing to handle the ribbons."

Rushmere's lip curled. "That is all very well, if one does not mind risking one's cattle to such inexperienced hands. But then Saunderton never has had much flair in his driving."

Miles might not indulge in the neck-or-nothing style favored by the marquis, but that did not signify a lack of ability. If anything, it indicated good sense. But she refrained from voicing that thought out loud. After all, it was not her part to defend that exasperating, managing man.

By the time they had completed their second round, they found that Ashby and Hanna Brookstone had arrived. Charles Dauntry walked his horse beside their curricle, and whatever he said sent Hanna off into a fit of the giggles from which she seemed to be having trouble recovering. Ashby, grinning broadly, waved at them. "We're all here," he called.

Phoebe glanced about, but saw no other vehicles. "I thought you were inviting others," she said. "I know Wolverhampton had planned—"

"Familial duties have claimed him, I fear." Rushmere didn't sound in the least disappointed. "And as for the others, I changed my mind." He directed that smile at her that her former pupils had found so devastating. "I didn't want to be distracted from you."

Phoebe had ample time to digest this comment, for the journey to Hampton Court took them almost two full hours. Rushmere complained about the slowness of the pace, but as this was primarily set by the anti-social behavior of his own leader, he could blame no one but himself. For most of the time he drove in silence, his attention entirely taken up by his team, which left Phoebe time to wonder at Xanthe's schemes. If Rushmere intended to make her an offer, it would be soon. But the question of *if* had begun to intrude itself into her mind.

By the time they approached their destination, Phoebe longed for nothing more than to climb down from the carriage. Once she returned safely to Half Moon Street, she vowed she would never again subject herself to so uncomfortable a journey. Rushmere possessed a very dashing curricle; she had seen it in Queen's Square on several occasions. What had ever possessed him to drive this contraption instead?

Rushmere glanced toward her. "We are about to enter the outer green court," he informed her.

Dutifully, Phoebe opened eyes she had closed against the queasiness caused by the swaying carriage. Expanses of impressive lawns stretched out around them, which she duly admired. Then they reached the bridge that allowed them to cross the moat, and they were passing through the magnificent gateway while the hoofbeats of their horses echoed back to her. Rushmere drew up before the palace's brick facade, with its buttresses and gilded vanes, and liveried servants poured forth from the doorway, taking charge of the party that clambered out of the vehicles lining up behind them.

Phoebe, faced with the precarious climb down from

her perch, hesitated. She looked toward Rushmere, but that gentleman had his back to her, speaking with a man who bore all the appearance of being a secretary with an army of royal servants clustering in his wake. Nor did the groom have time to spare for a petite young lady trapped atop the swaying equipage. He had already gone to the head of the lead horse, and stood talking to it in soothing tones. She was on her own.

Footsteps crunched on the gravel, and Sir Miles smiled up at her. "Stranded?"

She could think of nothing polite to say in response; she did not enjoy feeling quite so foolish. Having no choice, she permitted him to help her find unstable footing to lower herself a foot or two. But as she swayed, he caught her about the waist, lifting her easily from the carriage and setting her gently on the ground. For one long moment they stood with his hands cupped about her waist. A strange, troubled expression flickered in his eyes as he released her.

She stepped back, oddly breathless, and managed a husky "Thank you."

"My pleasure," he said, his tone tight, as if pleasure were most assuredly not the emotion he had experienced from their contact.

Rushmere ended his conversation, turned, and saw her. "Ah, Miss Caldicot. Shall we proceed?" He gestured toward the other members of their party, gathering them together before their guide, then withdrew a pace.

The gentleman introduced himself as Mr. Jennings, then launched into a history of the house from its origins in the twelfth century as a small manor in the hands of the Order of St. John of Jerusalem, its acquisition by Thomas, Cardinal Wolsey in 1514, and its inevitable passage into the hands of Henry VIII when Wolsey fell out of royal favor. Then the tour began in earnest, and Phoebe, on Rushmere's arm, wandered through a regular rabbit warren of halls, state apartments, bedchambers, drawing rooms, staircases and courtyards. Walls and ceilings alike boasted paintings and carvings, and panelings were pointed out with pride. A bewildering array of tapestries met the eye, and everywhere she looked she encountered more statuettes and porcelains. At last they entered a hall that Phoebe suspected they had visited before—their first stop, perhaps?—and Mr. Jennings turned to face them with welcome news.

"You will find refreshments set up in the gardens," he declared in the tone of voice of one concluding a lengthy task.

Rushmere thanked him, requested he convey his respects to a number of august personages, and led the way outside.

She'd been wrong, Phoebe realized. They had not entered by this hall. At least, they had not entered by this door. They now faced gardens, acres of greenery, formal flower beds, fountains, pools. Lost in admiration, Phoebe trailed along after the others to where linen-spread tables, heaped with covered platters and dishes, stood on an expanse of lawn, attended by no less than half a dozen liveried servants.

Phoebe partook sparingly of the innumerable, succulent dishes, her mind in a whirl. Had Xanthe arranged all this—or had Rushmere, alone and uninfluenced, planned the outing? She couldn't tell what to make of his manner, which varied from the flirtatious to the inattentive. She found it disconcerting, quite putting a pall over what might otherwise have been a delightful afternoon.

Ashby and Hanna Brookstone finished their meal and strolled off to enjoy the fifty acres of grounds. Lucilla followed them with her frowning gaze, then returned her attention to her serving of raspberry fool, but showed no pleasure whatsoever in the delicacy. An angry gleam showed in her eye that fascinated Phoebe. Under cover of a discussion between the other gentlemen at the table, Phoebe joined the girl.

"Hanna looks delightful in that sprigged muslin, does she not?" And if that didn't unleash Lucy's tongue, nothing would.

Lucy stabbed her spoon into the unoffending confection. "What can possess her to flirt so shockingly with Simon? I would never do so."

"No," Phoebe agreed. "But then you are probably the only young lady in London who wouldn't jump at the chance to do so."

Lucy blinked at her. "Whatever do you mean?"

Phoebe gave a soft laugh. "Have you not listened to the whisperings?"

"What whisperings?" the girl demanded, suspicious.

"That he is a matrimonial prize of the first water," came Phoebe's prompt response. "You need have no fear your brother will continue to pressure you into marrying him. Lord Ashby has any number of caps set for him. I have heard several young ladies saying they quite envy you for being upon such terms with him."

"Really?" Lucilla stared at her, but her gaze remained unfocused as if she saw something else entirely.

A footfall sounded behind Phoebe, and Rushmere appeared at her shoulder. He smiled, holding out his hand. "Should you care to stroll about the gardens?"

While she accompanied the marquis to examine a formal bed of roses, Dauntry and Miles collected Lucy. Over her shoulder, Phoebe glimpsed the three of them heading in the opposite direction, across the lawn toward the Wilderness, an area of trees, shrubs, and a multitude of paths. The famous maze, planted during the reign of William and Mary, lay in a corner of that vast area; Phoebe wanted to see it. But most of all, it dawned on her, she did not really wish to be alone with Rushmere.

She looked up and found his gaze resting on her, an unsettling gleam in his eyes. She moved a step away. "You have arranged a delightful day," she said, keeping her tone light.

He took her hand from his arm, carried it to his lips, then replaced it with a gentle caress. "It is not over, yet, my dear."

The look that accompanied that only increased Phoebe's sense of unease. What else had he planned? She moved a step away. "Will we have time to see the maze?" And this time it was she who led the way, in pursuit of the others.

She spotted Sir Miles in conversation with Hanna and Charles Dauntry near the entrance of the maze.

Lucy stood in pensive silence beside them, gazing at the massive hedge. Then the girl turned slowly, scanning the park land. She stiffened, and Phoebe looked in the same direction, in time to catch a glimpse of another person, a man in a scarlet coat.

Lieutenant Harwich. She hadn't a doubt about his identity. But how had he come to be here? He certainly had not been invited. He must have crept onto the grounds—but with Lucilla's knowledge, or on his own?

Rushmere ran his thumb along the back of her hand. "I should keep you amid the formal beds."

That jerked Phoebe out of her troubled reverie. She stopped and stared at him. "I beg your pardon?"

"Flowers." He smiled at her, supremely confident. "They would serve as a more proper setting for you than this Wilderness. You should be surrounded by flowers, delicate ones, violets or tulips."

She was in no mood to flirt, and it took an effort not to tell him so. But by then they had reached the others, and Miles cast her a quizzical look, giving her something new to worry about. Should she tell him about the presence of Lieutenant Harwich? Of course, she could not be absolutely certain it had been he she saw. For the moment, she decided, she would do best to say nothing.

Hanna, Dauntry and Miles headed into the maze, followed by Lucy, who seemed in no hurry. Phoebe started after them, but Rushmere held her back, his manner once more that of an attentive host. "Would you care to be given the key to the center?"

"Absolutely not!" she objected. "It would quite ruin the fun."

"Then, I shall leave you for a little to enjoy it. But never fear, I shall return to rescue you after you have become hopelessly lost." Holding her gaze, he kissed her hand, then headed back the way they had come.

Phoebe stared after him for a moment, then plunged between the yew walls. She could hear laughter and calls from various directions, indicating that the members of her party had wasted no time in becoming thoroughly lost. Left seemed an unlikely first direction, so she turned that way, then glanced back at the entrance to memorize how the passage looked from this direction. What she saw, though, was Lucilla slipping through the exit.

Phoebe didn't waste time pondering intents and purposes. She followed, and as she emerged from the shrubbery she was greeted by the unwelcome sight of Lucy's back as the girl hurried to reach the scarlet-coated officer who strode toward her. They met, clasping hands, and for a long moment simply stood gazing into one another's eyes. Then the officer seemed to recollect himself, and he drew Lucy away, across the Wilderness to vanish behind a hedge. Phoebe followed, but soon found herself amid a formal planting of flowers and shrubs with her quarry nowhere to be seen. She took a few more uncertain steps, then halted, staring about at a loss. Then a feminine giggle, from just behind the rhododendrons where she stood, reassured her. She circled around the leafy barrier and found herself in a secluded bower, facing the two truants.

Lieutenant Harwich, who sat upon a bench at Lucilla's side, sprang to his feet at once, his expression alarmed. Then he seemed to take in his diminutive confronter, and he straightened, his manner taking on a belligerent edge. He looked down on her from his superior height, and his lip curled. "You are intruding."

Lucy, though, did not take so sanguine an attitude to being discovered. She shrank back with a gasp, and her eyes widened. "Miss Caldicot! I—I thought you were in the maze."

"Be glad your brother is. Lieutenant Harwich, you must not be caught here. Hampton Court is not open to the general public, and I cannot but think Rushmere would not be pleased to discover his guest list has expanded itself without his consent."

Dull color flushed the lieutenant's face. "I needed to speak with Miss Saunderton," he said with an assumption of hauteur. "Urgently."

Phoebe eyed him coldly. "And now that you have done so, you may leave—and as quickly as possible, I would suggest."

He hesitated a moment, then turned to Lucilla and, taking her hands, pressed them. "Until later," he said. He awarded Phoebe a curt bow, then spun and strode away along the path.

Phoebe watched until he rounded a corner and vanished from sight, then turned back to Lucy, who stood now, watching her warily.

"Are you going to tell Miles?" she asked in a tone in which defiance faded beneath resignation.

"Should I?" Phoebe countered, then added in a rush,

"You really cannot keep meeting officers like this, Lucy. You will gain the most shocking reputation."

"Oh, how can you say such a dreadful thing! Why is it so terrible to speak to a gentleman?"

"Why do you need to seek out such privacy if your intentions are quite proper?" Phoebe shot back.

Lucy's color heightened. "It is only because he should not have come here."

"What did he have to say that could not wait a few more hours?"

Lucy's lips twitched, then spread into a secret smile. "He came simply because he was not invited. He is quite daring, and said he would prove that nothing would keep him from—" She broke off in consternation. "From—from seeing me if he wished," she finished lamely. "Oh, Miss Caldicot, there is truly no reason to tell Miles about this. There has been no harm done, and I told him it was wrong of him, truly I did."

Phoebe fixed her with her best schoolmistress expression. "Give me your word you will not slip off to meet him—or anyone else—in this manner again."

Lucy hung her head. "I promise."

Phoebe shook her head. "You have to mean it."

Lucy looked up, stung. "I—" she began, then broke off. "Very well," she said, resignedly. "I promise before I do anything, I shall ask myself whether or not you would approve, and then act as you would wish."

"If you mean that, then I suppose there is no need to tell your brother about this."

"Oh, thank you, Miss Caldicot!" Lucy flung her arms about her former preceptress, giving her an enthusiastic hug. "I always knew you were a darling.

Let us get back before they realize we are not lost in the maze."

With that plan, Phoebe heartily agreed. Lucy's promise did not completely relieve her mind, for she had a shrewd notion that Lucy might view potential indiscretions in a more tolerant light than would she, herself. But she knew she would get no more, and led the way back to where the sound of laughing voices assured them that the others had yet to penetrate to the heart of the maze.

By the time they, too, had become lost between the yew hedges, the shouts of triumph assured them that a solution was indeed possible. Lucy ran off, calling for directions that no one could possibly give, as they had no idea where, amid the winding passages, she raced. Phoebe strolled in the opposite direction, glad just to be alone.

It was not, she decided after a little while, that the maze was so very complex. It was simply so very large. The pathways took considerable time to traverse, so that when one found oneself facing a dead end, one had to return that great distance again. She turned a sharp corner, and found herself facing Rushmere.

"I wondered how long it would take you to get here," he said.

She had found the center. The others, she realized the next moment, had already gone. Rushmere took her hand, his thumb smoothing her palm, and she tried to draw back.

"We will not be disturbed," he said softly. "Saunderton has taken them to view one of the other gardens."

"They will wonder where we are." She inched away, trying to maintain the distance between them that he seemed bent on removing. And what, she wondered, was she doing? Xanthe was offering her a matrimonial prize of the first water in answer to her wish, and all she wanted was to escape. It made no sense whatsoever.

Rushmere eased another step nearer, and his hand clasped hers. "Nervous, Miss Caldicot?" His tone teased, but the gleam in his eyes warned her he was serious.

Indecision tore at her. If his intentions were dishonorable, then the matter needn't trouble her in the least. She had only to send him about his business. But what if his purpose was marriage, which she was inclined to believe it must be? Surely Xanthe wouldn't arrange anything less for her. Yet in spite of his exalted title and position, in spite of his dashing and flirtatious manner, in spite of her daydreams inspired by her pupils' rapturous whisperings about him, she didn't love him in the least. Yet did that matter when compared with the innumerable advantages of such a match, both for herself and for Thomas? All she had to do was stop retreating, let him kiss her, allow him to declare himself—

"Here you are." Miles's deep voice sounded behind her.

Relief washed over her, followed at once by indignation at his picking this, of all moments, to interrupt. Could he not even permit her to make this decision on her own?

"Have you been unable to find your way back out?"

he inquired, apparently oblivious to the tension that filled the air. He offered Phoebe his arm.

Rushmere tucked her hand firmly into his own arm. "I am well acquainted with the paths," he informed Miles, and drew her away from her would-be rescuer. The two gentlemen exchanged a long, measuring look; then the marquis strode down the path, pulling Phoebe with him.

She would have been content to return to Half Moon Street at once, but despite the advancing hour, Rushmere suggested they tour more of the gardens. Phoebe strolled along with him dutifully, responding to his flirtatious comments with a smile that grew progressively more rigid, and wishing for the long day to end. It had grown quite late when at last the marquis sent for the carriages, and the party began their drive home.

Phoebe cast one look of longing at Miles's wellsprung curricle, then resigned herself to the uncomfortable ride of Rushmere's vehicle. Exhausted from the long day, she clung to the carriage's side as the precarious phaeton pitched and swayed. At least he kept his team to a decorous pace rather than racing ahead. Ashby and Hanna, waving gaily, swept past them a mile or two beyond the gates of Hampton Court. Then Miles and Lucilla, with Charles Dauntry riding at their side, left them behind. For some time Phoebe could see their dust, but in the fading light of the late afternoon this soon vanished.

They continued at their steady, slow pace, the distance between them and the other vehicles growing greater and greater, until they reached the outskirts of a tiny inhabited area too small even for the designation of village. The phaeton lurched to a stop, its body swinging wildly, and Rushmere clambered down. Phoebe peered over the side as the marquis and his groom consulted.

"Damaged axle," Rushmere declared after a cursory examination of one of the wheels. He held up his arms, and Phoebe allowed him to help her from the vehicle.

"Will you have trouble getting it fixed?" she asked as he took her arm and led her up the road.

"No need for you to worry, my dear." He patted her hand. "There's an inn just a few steps away."

Phoebe hung back. "Is there also a blacksmith?"

"You need not worry," he repeated. He drew her along the road, past the first of the cottages.

There weren't many. The village didn't seem large enough to be able to provide more than an indifferent meal for a passing traveler. Surely, though, there must be at least a smithy. She cast an uncertain glance at an establishment that bore all the appearance of a common ale house. Still, if any gentleman of Rushmere's rank and taste were willing to stop here, it could not be as bad as she feared.

It was not. Inside, she found the floors and tables scrubbed, the innkeeper who greeted them respectable, and the maid who brought wine and cakes to be primly gowned. Almost, Phoebe reflected as she settled in the corner of the inn's only private parlor, as if they were accustomed to noblemen breaking down at their doorstep. But perhaps they were, situated so close to Hampton Court. She could only be grateful for her good fortune. While Rushmere, with a murmured word of excuse, departed to make his inquiries, Phoebe relaxed before the cozy fire, took another sip of wine, and gave up an unequal struggle and allowed her eyes to close.

How much time passed before the marquis returned, she had no way of knowing. She opened her eyes to find that candles now lit the tiny apartment, and outside the windows all seemed black. Rushmere stood in the room, his cloak and driving gloves cast across the back of a chair, a glass of the excellent wine in his hand.

He looked up as she stirred, and smiled. "So, you are awake, my dear."

She smothered a yawn. "I'll be with you in a moment, my lord."

"You are with me now," he pointed out, and settled himself in the chair opposite her.

She shook her head, rising. "We must be getting back. Lady Xanthe will be worried."

Rushmere studied his glass, his expression pensive. "I am afraid, my dear, that will be impossible."

"But—" She sank onto the chair again. "Why?"

"I fear the axle cannot be fixed until morning."

"Until—" She sat up straight, staring at him. "Until *morning?* Then, I shall have to hire a carriage, I suppose."

"There's no need." His smile sounded in his voice, and he reached across and took her hand. "This will give us the opportunity to continue the discussion we had barely begun when Saunderton showed the ill breeding to interrupt us in the maze. We have a great deal to discuss, you and I."

"Have we?" She pulled away, chilled. "I fear that will be impossible. I must return to London tonight. Will you arrange for the hiring of a carriage for me?"

He leaned back in his chair, his smile growing. "I fear there are no conveyances available."

"None at all?" Disbelief welled in her, only to fade into anger. The horrible suspicion dawned on her that there was not a thing wrong with that phaeton. He had plotted this with care, allowing the others to go ahead, stranding them in a place where it seemed impossible she could get help, still a good nine miles from London. Whether he in fact planned to offer her marriage or ruination, she discovered she honestly did not care. She didn't want anything to do with him. She looked about, fuming.

"You shall have to make the best of it," he said. So much self-satisfaction sounded in his voice, there could be no room for any trace of an apology. "You will find that can be very good, indeed."

"Will it?" She made a show of looking at her slippers. "Perhaps you are right. These seem to be quite stout shoes." And with that, she pulled free of his hold and stalked from the room, slamming the door behind her.

She had descended the stairs and stormed out into the gathering night before the enormity of her situation struck her. Well, she had done it this time. She had thrown away her chance at marriage with a marquis. If that had been Xanthe's answer to her wish—she shied from completing that thought. Her wish, her precious, wonderful wish, wasted. She had failed Thomas.

And if that weren't bad enough, she was probably about to lose her reputation as well. If that happened, she would never be able to find respectable employment, never be able to so much as assist her poor brother, never be able to support herself again. . . .

She was growing despondent, she realized.

But perhaps she had cause.

Eight

Before Phoebe reached the end of the village, she heard Rushmere's booted footsteps striding after her. She paid them no heed, except to increase her own pace. Still, he gained on her. He called her name, and she ignored him. That brought an audible exclamation of vexation from him, and his pace quickened. She, too, walked faster. It would be fully dark soon, and the last thing she wanted was to waste more time and words on the marquis.

Twenty strides later, his hand closed over her wrist. "Miss Caldicot," he said, his breath coming heavily, "you are behaving in a ludicrous manner."

"*I* am?" she cried, spinning to face him, unleashing her outrage at last. "Do you really think it is ludicrous to try to preserve my reputation?"

"Is that all that is worrying you?" His own vexation relaxed. "My dear girl—"

She turned on her heel and started walking once more. She didn't want to hear his explanations or excuses. She simply wanted to escape from him, from this whole, dreadful day. The chill breeze sent the ends of her thin shawl waving, and she shivered. Surely she wouldn't have to walk the whole distance back to London. There must be a farm where she could get help. Or barring that, there would be another village soon. She shrank from the inevitable explanations, from the fact that she carried but little money with her.

She could still hear him behind her. For how long would she have to endure this pursuit before she convinced him she had no intention of returning with him? She should never have encouraged his advances, never led him to believe she might be willing to accept a *carte blanche*. She'd been so certain this high-ranking nobleman must be Xanthe's answer—

The sound of an approaching carriage caught her attention, and for a moment her hopes soared. Only the vehicle came toward her, not headed for London. She moved over to the side of the road, not wanting to add being run down to her list of grievances for the day.

The carriage—a gentleman's curricle, pulled by a pair—slowed as it approached; then the horses eased from their trot to a walk, then a stop. The bay horses. The *familiar* bay horses. She transferred her gaze to the driver, and met the relieved gaze of Sir Miles Saunderton. He smiled, a warm, comforting expression, and Phoebe had to fight the absurd desire to burst into tears.

"I see I've found you at last," he said, quite unnecessarily. "We'd feared there'd been an accident when you didn't return. Are you safe?"

"We are quite all right, Saunderton." Rushmere glared at the new arrival.

"I am glad to hear it." Miles regarded the marquis

with a steady, challenging gaze that held more than a hint of deadly steel. "A high-perch phaeton can be dangerous. I would consider it a very grave matter if anything unpleasant befell Miss Caldicot."

Rushmere flushed. "You need not concern yourself for her safety."

"No." Miles held his gaze. "Not now, at least. Miss Caldicot, may I offer you a ride back to your god-mother? She is, needless to say, most concerned for you."

He picked up something from the seat and held it out to her: her pelisse, Phoebe realized with a rush of gratitude. She cast the flimsy shawl she had worn for the excursion to Hampton Court onto the seat of the carriage and donned the warmer garment against the growing cold of the approaching night. Now, if he'd only brought a rug and a hot brick, she would be quite in charity with him.

As soon as she had fastened her buttons, he held out his hand, and Phoebe grasped it, accepting his aid as she climbed into the curricle. Easy, compared to the high-perch phaeton, a vehicle she sincerely hoped she never laid eyes upon again. She settled at his side, and already he drew a rug from beneath the seat and spread it across her legs. She snuggled into it.

Miles took the ribbons in both hands. "Good evening, Rushmere," he said and gave his horses the office.

Phoebe glanced down at the outraged marquis. "Thank you, my lord, for a—a most interesting day," she said, her tone icy. And with that, she lapsed into a fuming silence as Sir Miles turned his equipage and headed back the way he had come.

They drove without speaking for some little time while the awkwardness of the situation struck her. She and Miles had barely spoken a civil word to one another over the last few days. Their last real encounter, in fact, had been a raging argument in which he had told her to stop meddling in Lucy's affairs. And now here he was, meddling in hers—and she could only be profoundly grateful that he had. Still, it made the situation a trifle sticky. With an effort, she managed, albeit stiffly, "I have not yet thanked you for coming."

He spared her an amused glance. "I imagine you have done much the same for Lucy on more than one occasion." He sounded unconcerned, as if journeying some nine miles, with horses already tired from the original expedition, were of no account.

"Nevertheless, I am grateful," she said, unbending a little.

"If you can refrain from catching a chill for another quarter of an hour, we will come to an inn where I have already bespoken several hot bricks."

"Oh!" A gasping chuckle escaped her. "You are bent upon making me beg your pardon for every unkind thought I have ever harbored against you."

"Well, if one tends to be of a managing disposition, one ought to put it toward a good cause."

At that, she actually laughed—something she could not have imagined doing half an hour before.

They arrived at the inn a short time later, and while the bricks were placed about her feet, the innkeeper himself handed her a steaming mug of mulled wine.

This she sipped as the horses trotted briskly out of the yard and resumed their journey to London. "I was right," she murmured as her eyelids began to droop. "It is well sprung." And with that she settled back in surprising comfort and allowed the strains of the day to fade away.

She roused some time later to the realization she had fallen asleep. The horses had slowed, and now they turned through a narrow gate. She sat up, and discovered she had been using Miles's shoulder as a pillow. "I beg your pardon—" she began, then broke off her apology. "Where are we?" she demanded, eyeing the illuminated windows of a manor house at the end of the drive.

"Westerly Place. The home of Mr. and Mrs. Pershing," he told her, his voice soothing. "No, I am not abducting you. Your godmother is here. We felt your arrival in Half Moon Street under these circumstances might give rise to unpleasant gossip. So you will attend a very small dinner party here, and then you and Lady Xanthe will return to your home in your own carriage. There will be no hint of impropriety attached to the evening."

"That," she said after a moment, "sounds like your managing again."

"Mea culpa," he agreed, his amusement sounding in his voice.

"There are times," she said, as one admitting to an unwelcome truth, "when a bit of managing does not come amiss. But how did you know I needed rescuing?"

He cast her a sideways glance as they drew up before the house. "I guessed. Forgive me, but Rushmere can be rather obvious at times."

"And I can be rather dense," she said in a very small voice.

"Not that I have ever seen." He jumped down and came around to her side. "But I should have to say it was your own uneasiness in his company that alerted me to the possibility that his intentions might prove to cause you some little difficulty this night."

"A little," she admitted. She accepted his hand, and he helped her to alight.

A groom ran up from a path leading around the corner of the house, and Miles handed the bays over into the man's charge. He turned back to Phoebe, offering her his arm. "When you did not return within an hour of our own arrival, I thought it best to set out in search of you."

"And to involve my—my godmother in your scheme?"

"She was quite delighted with it, I assure you. Kept humming to herself."

"Humming?" Phoebe demanded, her gaze narrowing. "Now, I wonder what she was up to?" But as she added this last in an undervoice, Miles might not have heard.

The front door swung open as they approached, and he led her up the stairs and into a small but elegantly appointed entry hall. Phoebe barely had a chance to look around her before she found herself facing a footman who waited to relieve her of her pelisse and bonnet. Freed of these garments, she allowed Miles to escort her across the hall and into a salon.

An elderly couple sat side by side on a sofa before a hearth, and Xanthe sat in a chair facing them, sipping from a wineglass. The sweet smell of almonds and lemon filled the room, stirring Phoebe's hunger. Her relief at seeing her godmother faded beneath a burning desire for the answers to a few questions, but she held these in check while Miles introduced her to her host—a small, rotund man with thinning white hair and twinkling blue eyes—and hostess—a spare woman with silvery hair and the sweetest expression Phoebe had ever beheld.

"And now, my love," said Xanthe, "we must make you more comfortable. If you will excuse us?" She directed a brilliant smile toward the others and swept Phoebe from the room.

Phoebe cast a glance over her shoulder at Miles, then followed her godmother, determined to have a few words with her in private. As soon as the housekeeper had shown them to a bedchamber, ascertained they had all they needed, and taken her departure, Phoebe rounded on Xanthe. "What have you been about?" she demanded.

"With Rushmere?" Xanthe did not pretend to misunderstand. "Not a single thing, my love."

Phoebe blinked at her. "But—it was because of you he paid me such attentions. Why else would he look at me?"

"For your own sake, child. I had no hand in that."

Phoebe sank onto the edge of the bed. "I thought it was your doing. I thought you offered him to me as the answer to my wish."

Xanthe settled beside her, taking her hand. "I only

offer opportunities, my love. Only you can provide the answers."

"I see." A wry smile tugged at Phoebe's lips. "To think I set my cap for him simply because I felt I *had* to. I was so afraid of ruining the—the *opportunity* you gave me. Only it wasn't him at all."

"It could be anyone, my love, whomever your heart leads you to. Or it could be no one. It is entirely up to you, and what you truly desire."

Phoebe rose and paced across the floor. "I want Thomas to finish his education," she said after a long couple of minutes.

"Very admirable," approved Xanthe. "But that has nothing to do with what you want for yourself." Phoebe stopped and stared at her, and Xanthe smiled that mysterious smile. "You have never given that aspect sufficient thought, have you, my love?"

Phoebe found she had no answer for that.

Xanthe's eyes gleamed. "Shall we join the others now?"

"I have to change my—" Phoebe began, only to break off as she looked down at her gown. The crumpled muslin of the day had vanished, to be replaced by a low-cut evening gown of amber-colored silk, decorated with only a single ruffle at the hem. She turned to the mirror that hung above the dressing table, and discovered that her hair now hung in heavy ringlets from a knot at the crown of her head, while wisping tendrils framed her face. A strand of amber beads clasped about her throat.

"Magic," said Xanthe with a note of smugness, "can certainly be useful, can it not?" She rose, took

Phoebe's arm, and led her toward the door. "As long as you remember it cannot solve every problem."

They descended the stairs to find Miles and the elderly Pershings still in the salon, surrounded by papers that on closer inspection proved to be musical scores. As they entered, Miles came to his feet, his gaze resting on Phoebe with a look she couldn't quite fathom. It left a warming glow in her, though. Almost at once a portly butler of kindly aspect announced dinner, and they crossed the hall to the dining room, a small apartment furnished with comfort rather than grandeur in mind. Phoebe liked it at once.

She took the seat Miles held for her. As he settled at her side, she looked up at him and said softly, "Thank you." He touched her hand, a fleeting contact, but the smile that accompanied it filled her with an unexpected contentment.

A nosegay of violets erupted into the air before her, and their petals cascaded down to her plate, vanishing before they touched the china. She looked up quickly and saw similar petal showers falling over the other members of the party. Xanthe met her accusing gaze with a mischievous wink, and the petals reappeared, swirling upward to burst into iridescent particles as they collided with the ceiling.

The strains of a string quartet sounded in her mind. Xanthe humming? she wondered, but her godmother addressed her hostess, her attention apparently far from music. The magic, though, continued. Even the candles seemed to burn with a warmer hue, casting a rosy-golden glow over the table, the courses presented by the butler, the wine that sparkled in the crystal glasses.

Talk centered around music, of Mr. Pershing's search for a viola of exquisite quality, of the discovery of a new musical score arranged for a quartet, and of altering favorite arrangements for fewer instruments as so very few people really enjoyed sitting down to an evening of serious music these days. In the midst of this, Mrs. Pershing turned to Xanthe. "Do you by any chance play? So foolish of me to hope, I know, but it has been so very long." She blinked wide, hopeful eyes.

"By happy chance," said Xanthe, her eyes brimming with mischief, "Sir Miles mentioned we might indulge ourselves this night. I have brought my flute with me."

Mrs. Pershing radiated joy. "And Miss Caldicot? Can we hope that she, too, is musically inclined?"

"She plays the pianoforte," Miles assured his old friend. "Exceptionally well, I might add."

This accolade startled Phoebe, but she had no time to dwell on its unexpectedness. Already the eager Mrs. Pershing rose from the table, not allowing the gentlemen to linger over brandy, but ushering them to the music room where she took a violin lovingly from its case. Her husband turned to his viola, and Miles bent to examine the cello that stood in a corner, wrapped in protective cloths.

While the Pershings sorted through various scores, Phoebe moved to Miles's side. "You and your friends have gone to a great deal of trouble for me this night."

"Not in the least." His smile held a touch of amusement. "I fear they will now make you play for your supper. I hope you are not too tired."

She shook her head. "I am actually looking forward to it. But I have had little opportunity to play with a group like this. I hope I won't disgrace myself."

Miles's eyes gleamed in the candlelight. "You couldn't," he said simply, and turned his attention to tuning his borrowed instrument.

After the first few faltering, tentative notes, Phoebe lost herself in the joy of playing with gifted companions. She could imagine nothing more unlike teaching bored young ladies the rudiments of the pianoforte. They launched into another piece, this one a sonata unfamiliar to her, and she quickly discovered it was of Mr. Pershing's own composing when he broke off in the middle of a run of sixteenth notes and announced he must make a change.

Miles laid his cello aside. "This will take some time," he informed Phoebe. "Would you care to stroll in the garden while we wait?"

As Xanthe and Mrs. Pershing embarked on an impromptu duet at that moment, Phoebe rose and accompanied Miles toward the drapes on the far side of the room. She'd never seen him so relaxed; the change in him fascinated her. Or did she merely choose to see him without the eyes of prejudice this night? He drew back the curtain to reveal French windows, which he opened, and she stepped out beneath a shaggy rose arbor arching high on its trellis.

Moonlight flooded the garden, and a surprisingly warm breeze brought the heady scent of the huge blossoms, along with gardenia and violet. Other flowers blended their aromas, creating an intoxicating perfume. She could hear water babbling softly from the depths of a nearby stream, and above, in a sky of midnight blue velvet, myriad stars glimmered with a rainbow of light. Violet, brilliant pale-yellow, icy blue—the intensity of the colors penetrated, and she realized Xanthe added her mite to the beauty of the night. She wasn't the least bit surprised to see half a dozen tiny fairies dancing about on the moonlit grass, nor another half dozen plying miniature musical instruments. She cast a surreptitious glance at Miles, but he seemed oblivious to the exotic touches to his surroundings.

He led the way along a flagstone path, between lavender shrubs and hollyhocks, until they reached a bench set against a wall of hawthorn. She seated herself, knowing she had not the least worry about staining her gown, and he joined her, leaning back to look up at the sky.

"One should always escape to a garden whenever one has worries," he said.

"This is certainly a perfect one," she agreed, a touch dryly.

A cat emerged from beneath the hawthorn, gleaming pale in the moonlight. For one moment, Phoebe thought it was Titus; then it leapt to her lap, and she realized this was a smaller feline, pale cream in color. And it lacked that smug, supercilious expression. She stroked its fur, and it set up a rhythmic purring.

"You are honored." Miles sounded amused. "Hannibal does not favor everyone."

"That was one of the many disadvantages of the

Misses Crippenham's Academy." Phoebe rubbed an ear, to the cat's intense satisfaction. "I could not keep either a cat or a dog."

"A grave disadvantage," he agreed. "Everyone needs a puppy to chew one's slippers or savage one's best waistcoat."

"You have had one, I see."

"Mmmm. Though they're not half the trouble of some sisters." He turned to gaze lazily down at her. "And what of you? Have you any siblings? I don't remember you speaking of any."

Which was hardly surprising, because until these last few minutes, they had scarcely exchanged a civil word. "My brother Thomas is up at Cambridge," she admitted, and at the thought of him couldn't prevent the smile that came to her lips.

"And you have been supporting him." It was a statement, not a question.

"Only helping," she said quickly. "He tutors."

Miles's brow snapped down. "That cannot cover the half of his expenses."

"They aren't as great as they might be. He lives very quietly, which he says is excellent training for when he becomes a curate and won't have two pennies to rub together."

His frown deepened. "Is he suited for the church, or can he think of no other profession?"

Phoebe shook her head, smiling. "I should say he is suited for nothing else."

She had been hearing the melodic notes of the flute and violin since they had come outside. Now, they broke into a familiar waltz melody. She caught herself humming it, and when Miles stood and held out his hand to her, it seemed the most natural thing in the world to take it. Hannibal sprang from her lap, and she rose to glide into the first of the open steps.

Lucilla had a point, Phoebe reflected as she looked up at Miles, aware of the play of shadow and moonlight on the planes and angles of his face. A touch of romance added something to one's existence, gave one's heart a reason to beat faster, one's breath to come more quickly, one's flesh to tingle with the contact. She allowed the music to flow over and through her, breathed in the sweet scents of the garden. Awareness swept over her, of his eyes, his smile, of the intangible bond that seemed to link them as surely as did his touch. When he gathered her into his arms for the circling steps, she melted against him, losing herself in the overwhelming sensations he created in her. He released her all too soon into the open movements, then pulled her close once more. And all the while his hand warmed hers in a clasp so perfect it seemed impossible to break it.

The music ended, and from within the house came the sound of voices. For a long moment they stood together, their hands still touching. Then he led her back to the bench and settled at her side, his gaze still holding hers. Slowly, he lifted one finger to touch her cheek, then brush tendrils of hair back from her face.

In another moment, the hazy thought filtered into her mind that he might kiss her. A thrill of yearning enveloped her, and her hand stole to his arm, just touching his sleeve; but the more reasoned portion of her brain warned her none of this was real, that it was all a Xanthe-induced fairy tale. She didn't want to succumb to a make-believe romance. What if Miles didn't truly want this? He couldn't, not judging from their previous encounters. Yet she longed for his touch, to feel his arms about her, to taste his kiss, so desperately it caused a physical ache within her.

"Phoebe." He breathed her name, making it a caress.

She couldn't allow it, couldn't let him do something he would regret. It took every ounce of her will to force herself to rise, and once on her feet, she found herself alarmingly unsteady. "Forgive me, I seem to be somewhat exhausted by the events of today. It would be best if we returned home soon. And I must thank you again for coming to my rescue." She gave him a wavering smile, then turned and hurried into the house.

As she came through the curtains, the Pershings looked up from the table where they examined a newly edited violin score. Xanthe laid aside her silver flute and rose. "My dear, there you are at last. It is time we took our leave."

Phoebe managed to express her thanks to Mr. and Mrs. Pershing for their hospitality, then found herself ushered outside to where Xanthe's coach already stood waiting. She started to climb in, but knew Miles was there, watching her. She longed to turn back, to run to him, to feel the strength and security of his embrace, but she could not, not when so much magic lingered in the air, influencing them both. Yet her gaze sought him where he stood on the steps, staring after her. She looked away, her eyes blurring, and settled on the rear seat, fighting the tears that threatened to overflow.

She was tired, that was all. She'd spent a long, eventful day, knowing worry and fury and fear. And then Miles had come. It was only natural she had overreacted to his capable and reassuring presence, to his masterful management of a terrible situation. She was grateful, that was all. And if Xanthe hadn't intervened with her romantic setting, they might have settled into a comfortable friendship. Instead—

No, she was too tired to sort out what had happened between them instead. Or had anything at all? Had it just been in her imagination? What would he have said had she allowed him to speak?

No, she'd been right to prevent him from saying words that owed their origin to a romantic setting provided by Xanthe. When he spoke—*if* he spoke—she had to be certain the words came from his own heart.

And what about her heart?

Too many questions remained unanswered, and right now exhaustion kept her from thinking clearly. Tomorrow, she promised herself. She would ride early, encounter him in the cold light of early morning reality, and see if the magic still lingered. If it did . . .

She cast a suspicious glance at her fairy godmother, but Xanthe appeared to have fallen asleep.

Nine

In the end, Phoebe did not ride in the park the next morning. Her muddled feelings confused her, and she didn't want to see Miles with her mind in this uncharacteristic chaos. She longed for exercise, to focus herself on controlling a difficult mount, anything that might help restore order to her disordered thoughts. She needed to know what had prompted the tenderness of his touch, of his voice, what lay in his heart.

But mostly, she needed to know what lay in her own.

She paid a round of morning visits with Xanthe, but found no diversion in talk of the ball that would be held that evening at Evanridge House. Miles would be there; she could not possibly avoid him. Of course, she probably need have no fear. She could count on him to behave as the gentleman he was, and give not the least sign of the emotional upheaval that had occurred.

He might not even be aware of it; it might all have occurred in her own imagination.

She still hadn't come to any certain answer to that question by the time their carriage pulled up in

Cavendish Square that night. As she entered the ball-room, already filled with the elite of the *ton,* she wondered for a moment if Xanthe had been at work, enhancing the decor. But her fairy godmother claimed complete innocence, leaving Phoebe to wonder at the dazzling gleam of the chandeliers, the flickering of myriad candles, the silks, satins, laces and jewels that everywhere met the eye. Her own gown, an amber silk underdress with a half robe of blond lace, had arrived only that morning from Madame Bernadette, and Phoebe secretly believed that even Xanthe could not have created anything more beautiful.

Would Miles like it? Suddenly, she had to know. Her anxious gaze searched the crowded room, until she spotted him, tall and elegant, less than twenty feet away. She could just glimpse the unmistakable dark head with the thickly gleaming waves of hair. If she went to him, would his eyes light with that warm smile that had caused her such confusion last night? Would he ask her to dance, perhaps a waltz so he could take her once more in his arms?

For the past several weeks, she reminded herself, she had hated him, blamed him for all her troubles. And now? She couldn't answer that, not yet. Nor did she dare approach him in so crowded a place, where her uncertainty might betray her to so many gossip-minded observers.

She dragged her gaze away from him and went in search of Xanthe, who had continued her progress along the wall, skirting the chairs placed for the chaperons. She found her near the refreshment table, regarding with a gleam of mischief in her violet eyes a lady of regal bearing and haughty countenance. Xanthe, it seemed, had been enjoying herself, for the ostrich feathers that made up the lady's head now drooped below her shoulders. Even as Phoebe watched, the plumes changed to vivid colors and began to sway in time to Xanthe's humming.

Xanthe, her expression not quite prim, turned to Phoebe. "A glass of champagne punch, my love? I believe you will enjoy it." She gestured toward the table, on which stood a giant bowl.

Phoebe peered into it, her suspicions aroused—and with cause. Xanthe's hum changed to a lilting tune, and a tiny frigate appeared, its sails billowing in a nonexistent wind. A miniature cannon fired at a floating orange segment, which exploded in an array of sparkling lights. Phoebe cast a rapid glance about, but no one, not even the footman who stood on duty behind the table, seemed to notice. With a sense of relieved appreciation, she watched the ship take aim at another segment, which went the way of the first.

Charles Dauntry claimed her for the reel that formed, and she moved easily onto the floor, relaxing in his undemanding company. She had never seriously considered him a suitor, she realized, despite his frequent visits and flattering attentions. She felt no temptation to do so now, either. Tonight she would not think about her wish, about her need to make the most of her opportunity to find a husband. Her determination to do that had nearly brought her to ruin. Tonight she would simply enjoy herself.

The lively dance ended, but Ashby intercepted them before they left the floor, begging the honor of leading her into the country dance that would form next. She accepted with pleasure, recognizing his company as another respite from worry. Nor was she mistaken. Each time the movements brought them together, he had some ready joke or droll comment on his lips concerning his cousin Lady Wrexham's litter of King Charles spaniel puppies, and soon had her laughing. It was with regret that she heard the music end, and took his arm to go in search of refreshment.

The miniature ship no longer inhabited the punch bowl; in its place swam a sea serpent, its long, slender body coiling in and out of the liquid, its scales iridescent, its eye winking at her. On one of the coils rode a miniature Xanthe, wings extended, waving gaily. Phoebe watched in fascination as the footman, oblivious to the bowl's occupants, ladled out glass after glass of the sparkling beverage.

Lucy, dragging Charles Dauntry with her, hurried over to join them, then stopped, eyeing Ashby with an uncharacteristic hesitation. The gentlemen exchanged cheerful greetings; then Ashby raised his quizzing glass and leveled it at Lucy. "Don't you look all the crack," he said, grinning in appreciation.

A soft flush touched Lucy's cheeks, but she preened for him, holding out the skirts of her sea green muslin for his further admiration. "I have received six compliments so far," she told him.

"Brat," he laughed. "You will become quite conceited."

"Impossible." She shook her head. "I shall always have you and Miles to assure that I do not. One or the other of you is always ready to make some odious comment to me. How is that new colt working out?" she added.

His smile broadened. "He's turning into the sweetest goer," he assured her. "If you behave, I might let you ride him some day."

"He's the one who will have to behave," the girl declared. "I'm glad he's working out, since you were so keen on him. It's a pity he's so very plain, though."

"Plain?" Ashby bridled. "That shows how little you know about horses! He's a regular high-bred 'un," he declared, and the two were off on one of their long-standing arguments.

Viscount Wolverhampton claimed her for a round dance, and as they took their place on the floor, a feather drifted down, hovered a moment before her face, then continued to the ground. A rounded feather, almost translucent, with golden tips. She looked up and saw Xanthe, still in that impossibly tiny size, perched on a chandelier. Her godmother waved again, then gestured toward where a sextet of strings and winds provided the music. The flautist, Phoebe noted in consternation, had taken on the appearance of a white horse.

With difficulty, Phoebe returned her attention to Wolverhampton as the dance began. In the next set, Lucy and Ashby took their belated places. Their argument, it seemed, had ended—or at least been postponed until later. It dawned on her that she had not seen Lieutenant Gregory Harwich this night. If he were not present, then Lucy would not be drawn into any unseemly behavior. Miles, she reflected, must be relieved.

Miles. She hadn't seen him since that glimpse when they had first arrived. He hadn't asked her to dance. An uncomfortable emptiness seeped through her. Did he avoid her? Perhaps he regretted the intimacy they had shared the previous night.

She looked about quickly, searching for him. Perhaps his aunt kept him by her side. But although a gentleman did occupy the chair next to Mrs. Mannering, his hair showed gray, and his slight build could never be confused with Miles's muscular bulk. She recognized him as Mr. Colney, who had played the oboe at their musical *soiree.*

She circled the viscount with the requisite slow, stately step, and there was Miles across the room, dancing with a rather plain, fair lady in an insipid pale blue gown. She'd seen them together before, had heard their calm, rational conversation. Lady Sophia Langley, she recalled. This seemed the perfect dance for such an unanimated young woman. She could not imagine what Miles saw in her to please him. Or perhaps it was Lady Sophia's very lack of independent ideas that appealed to him.

Miles and his partner separated in the next movement, and he took Hanna Brookstone's hand for a short promenade. Phoebe returned her attention momentarily to the gentleman whose hand she had just taken, then looked back to Miles. He said something to Hanna that made the girl laugh; then he returned her to Charles Dauntry, and the look that gentleman directed at Hanna caused Phoebe to miss a step, and drew a laughing rebuke upon her from Wolverhampton.

Hanna and Charles Dauntry? She caught another glimpse of them and saw the adoring expression on the girl's face which looked up into his. Hanna and Charles Dauntry, indeed. He must be at least eight years her senior! But of affable temperament and kindly disposition, she reminded herself. He was also a leader of fashion, and Hanna had always an eye for a gentleman's social position. Yet there were several present, younger than Dauntry, with titles and address sure to please the most exacting of ladies. Hanna had flirted with them without showing preference for any one over the others, until she'd met Dauntry.

Phoebe felt a pang of compassion for Hanna's poor mama. The woman had dragged her daughter to town in the hopes of snatching Rushmere for her before Phoebe could bring him up to scratch. After the dazzling prospect of a marquis, a mere honorable would seem a dreadful come-down. Yet Dauntry was by far the better man, and she could only hope Mrs. Brookstone could be brought to realize it.

The dance ended, and Wolverhampton led her from the floor. He paused for a moment to exchange a greeting with a friend, and Phoebe continued, looking about for anything absurdly out of place that would indicate where she might find Xanthe. As she peered through the crowd, the knots of people shifted, and there came Rushmere himself, walking directly toward her.

Anger and embarrassment collided within her, leaving her with no idea what to do or say. She could not make a scene in the middle of a ball, that much she knew. Discretion, she decided, dictated retreat. She spun about on her heel, and found herself staring at a familiar emerald stick pin stuck in the snowy folds of a simple but elegantly tied neckcloth.

Oh, the devil!

She allowed her gaze to travel upward, past the stiffly starched shirt points of moderate height, past the newly scraped chin so square and stubborn, past the firm mouth with the corners crooked upward into a heart-wrenching smile, past the classical nose and into eyes that glowed more amber than green. Their light faded, and his jaw tensed as his gaze focused beyond her. She glanced over her shoulder to see Rushmere frozen, staring back at Miles with an expression of mixed resentment and alarm on his face. This vanished beneath a mask of indifference. The marquis gave a short nod, then strolled off at a slight tangent.

Miles stared after him for a long moment, as if making sure the man had no intention of returning. Then he transferred his gaze to Phoebe, and smiled once more. "Are you free for this dance?" He offered his arm, and she took it.

She had expected to feel nothing but embarrassment in his company, yet she found she welcomed the solidity of his support. Without any trace of the awkwardness she had expected, she said, "He could not have dared approach me."

"It is possible he was as disconcerted to see you in his path as you were to see him," Miles suggested. "Or perhaps he wished to apologize."

"I should not have listened!" she exclaimed.

"Quite right." Miles nodded, his amusement returning. "One should not encourage mushrooms."

An unsteady laugh broke from her. "You are abominable," she informed him.

He awarded her a sweeping bow as he positioned her in the set. "It's heartening to have one's efforts appreciated."

In the next set, Lucy took her place with an all-too-familiar gentleman in a scarlet coat. Phoebe stiffened; he must have arrived only minutes before, and just when she'd hoped for an evening without his presence. She cast an anxious glance at Miles and saw his scowl.

This changed to a lopsided smile as he met her gaze. "You see I do nothing." He took her hand for the opening movement of the dance. "At least I shall give her no cause to think herself a martyr."

She circled the lady who stood diagonally to her, then returned to her position as Miles repeated the movement with the other gentleman. The reasonableness of his tone and manner surprised her. She mused on this as she took the hand of the gentleman opposite and circled with him, then faced Miles, her hand raised, palm to his palm.

The contact sent an unexpected thrill through her. She looked up, apprehensive, and met his steady gaze; his eyes, she noted as they walked slowly about one another, had gone deep green, as dark as a storm-tossed sea, impenetrable. The music, the other people who crowded the room, even conscious thought faded into the background. Only he seemed real, and she, anchored to him by that touch as soft as a whisper, as binding as a silken cord.

The dance continued. They separated, came back together, separated once more; yet she would swear they remained linked together. Even when they were at a distance, she felt the warmth of his touch lingering on her hand, the power of his presence wrapping about her. Awareness of him filled her, until even breathing seemed extraneous.

And he, did he feel the same? They came together once more, and she looked up into his eyes to see their gleam no longer rested on her. She followed the direction of their frowning gaze, and saw Lucy with Lieutenant Harwich, the girl staring at her companion with the oddest expression on her face. Phoebe looked away, feeling as if she intruded. Did Lucy, too, feel that nothing on earth mattered but the man with whom she danced?

Miles glanced down at her, his expression somber. "How does one make a child of her inexperience realize that an infatuation is not a good basis for a marriage?"

A shaky sigh escaped Phoebe, and when next they came together, she said, "Especially when she is convinced she has formed a lasting passion."

Miles's lips twitched into a wry smile. "Lord, I feel ancient and staid and far too sensible."

Phoebe nodded. "It is almost enough to make one long to do something rash, just to prove one has not settled into old age."

A deep, unexpected chuckle sounded from him. "Almost," he agreed.

Their palms came together once more as they circled, and that longing filled her, to forget her responsibilities, to forget her fears, to be reckless and laughing, just once. But the music ended, and he was thanking her, and she knew the opportunity had slipped through her fingers.

As he bowed over her hand, he asked, "Do you ride in the morning?"

Well, why not be reckless? she reflected. She offered what she hoped was a beguiling smile. "Do you?"

"What are you about?" A spark of interest lit his eyes.

"I thought perhaps you might care to drive, instead."

"Did you?" The spark increased to a gleam. "Now, why would you think that?"

"Because you wish to do something reckless."

He looked disappointed. "Driving my bays could hardly be considered an act of recklessness."

"It would, if you were to show me how to handle the ribbons."

"To show—" A smile tugged at the corner of his mouth. "My dear Miss Caldicot, might I have the honor of giving you a driving lesson?"

"You do not have to," she declared, suddenly conscience-stricken. "It is only that I saw you letting Lucy drive the other day, and you seemed so patient with her."

"I would be honored." He bowed over her hand. "At eight, then?" And with that, he left her.

She did not have the opportunity to speak with him again that night, and she feared he might forget. But at eight the following morning when she hurried outside, she found the curricle, with the two neat-stepping bays harnessed to it, waiting before the door. As she started to descend the steps, the neighboring door opened, and Miles appeared on the porch.

"Punctual, as always, I see," he said, smiling, and joined her at the vehicle. He handed her up, climbed in on the other side, then showed her how to hold the ribbons and how much contact to keep with the horses' mouths.

The pressure of his gloved hands on hers proved a considerable distraction, but she forced herself to concentrate. Not for worlds would she cause these gorgeous animals distress by hauling on their heads or giving conflicting signals. And not for worlds would she earn Miles's disapproval.

The early morning traffic set the bays skittering, and Miles resumed control. So effortlessly he managed the pair; now that she'd had a chance to feel the pull of two horses, rather than just one as when she rode, she could better appreciate his skill and the ease with which he communicated with the pair. She sat in silence, watching his deft hands as he eased the horses through the carts and wagons that went about their early business.

At last, they turned through the gates into the safety of the park, and Miles offered her the ribbons once more. She took them, and under his patient tutelage they completed their first round in far better style than they began it. By the end of the third round, she won a warm, "Well done!" from him, and that simple praise filled her with a glow that lasted until they returned to Half Moon Street.

He escorted her to her door, but refused her offer of refreshment, saying he had an appointment for which he already ran the risk of being late. He took her gloved hand, and for a moment she thought he might kiss it, despite the soft kid leather; but he merely pressed it, then strode up the steps to his own home. Phoebe entered the house, her thoughts lingering on the touch of his hand, the gentleness of his voice, his calm patience as he explained—for a second or even third time—the fine points of backing a pair or looping a rein.

Patience, yes. But had there been anything more? Any warmth, any hint that he might be forming a *tendre* for her? And what did she feel for him? The stirrings of infatuation? That didn't seem likely. She wouldn't describe her feelings as violent, not at all the emotion that beleaguered poor Lucy. What she felt was more comprehensive than friendship, more solid than mere liking, as a happiness held deep within. Or at least it would be a happiness if she thought it might be reciprocated.

She still puzzled over this when a tentative knock sounded on the front door. Absentmindedly, she opened it to find Lucy standing on her doorstep. The girl's eyes were red-rimmed from crying, and her cheeks betrayed an unnatural pallor.

"I am not a fool, am I?" the girl demanded by way of greeting.

Phoebe, dragged from her reverie, hushed her and ushered her into the front salon. James, the younger footman, hesitated in the hall, and Phoebe sent him for refreshment. She stripped off her gloves and riding hat, then turned her attention to the girl who stared at her, wide-eyed, her jaw set in a firm line. Lucilla bore a disconcerting resemblance to Miles at his most stubborn at this moment.

"What has happened?" Phoebe demanded, ignoring Lucy's opening gambit.

"Miles—beast that he is!—has called me foolish!" She sniffed.

"And what reasons did he give?"

Lucy sprang from the chair she had taken. "Because I will not wed Ashby."

Phoebe nodded. "Very wise of you. A most dissolute gentleman, who holds you in contempt. It is quite impossible to imagine you being happy with such a man."

"He is no such thing!" Lucy protested. "He is one of my dearest friends, and always has been. Only I cannot believe he loves me, for he—he called me *brat,* and he is forever in Hanna's company. And even if he did love me," she added hastily, "I could not possibly marry him when I am in love with someone else."

"Lieutenant Harwich." Phoebe nodded. "And he, of course, loves you and would never dangle after any other female."

"Well, he wouldn't." Lucy studied her clasped hands. "He loves me passionately, and says if I do not marry him he will kill himself."

Phoebe bit back the caustic remark that sprang to her lips. Instead, she asked, "Does a declaration such as that make you happy?"

"Oh, you do not understand, either!" Lucy cried.

"He is quite the most romantic gentleman I have ever met, so very dashing. How can I help but love him?"

Yet Phoebe thought she caught a note of hesitation in the girl's voice. "Every young lady longs for romance," Phoebe assured her. "It is a great pity that the gentlemen who are the most romantic, who display such passion when they pay one court, so often make the most uncomfortable of husbands."

Lucy glared at her. "You sound just like Miles."

"No, do I?" That stopped Phoebe. "I most sincerely beg your pardon."

A fleeting smile tugged at Lucy's lips. "And so you should. But why must we ladies be forced to choose between comfort and excitement in a husband? I want both!" She tilted her head to one side, regarding Phoebe with the air of one who had been—and in many ways still was—one of her pupils. "What do you think of Lieutenant Harwich, Miss Caldicot?"

Dismay filled Phoebe, and frantically she sought for just the right note so as to neither alienate nor encourage the girl. After a moment, she hazarded, "I do not believe I am well enough acquainted with him to give you a true answer. I know what is said of him, of course—"

Lucy sniffed. "Nothing that is good, I will wager."

"That is not exactly true." Phoebe weighed her words with care. "He is generally held to be handsome, and there are those who are pleased with his manners—"

"Miles is not one of them," Lucy inserted.

"I have observed his behavior," Phoebe plowed on, determined not to allow Miles and his opinions to enter into this discussion, "and while I can see the romantic aspect of many of the things he has done, I can also see—because I am not emotionally involved—where he gives his critics cause to disparage his conduct as dishonorable. No, Lucy." She held up her hand to stop the girl's protest. "One must be able—and willing—to view a person or situation from all points of view before one can truly form an opinion. His impetuous behavior has earned him his unsavory reputation."

Lucy sighed. "It does not matter to anyone whether he is judged fairly or not, does it?"

"Very little, I fear," Phoebe agreed.

Lucy paced the length of the room and back, her brow creased. As she passed Phoebe, she looked up and said, "Miss Caldicot, I—" then broke off. "I want to thank you," she finished lamely. "I believe I understand my brother a little better." Then impulsively, she went forward in a rush, gave Phoebe a brief but fervent hug, and hurried from the room.

Phoebe followed in time to see the girl let herself out to the street. She stood for a long while staring at the door, then went in search of Xanthe.

She found her in her room, with Titus curled on the bed watching as Xanthe tried on hats by the simple expedient of humming, then considering the resultant creation.

Xanthe looked up from beneath a straw bonnet with a silk-lined, high poke, which promptly turned into a cap of lace knotted with trailing violet ribands. "There you are, my dear," her godmother exclaimed. "Do you come with us this afternoon?"

"With you?" Phoebe wracked her memory. "Where?"

"Mrs. Weaver's. It is almost as far from London as Hampton Court, only in the opposite direction. I cannot recommend it, but you are quite welcome to join us."

"Us?" Phoebe raised her eyebrows. "You and Titus?"

Xanthe laughed. "Now, that would quite make the afternoon a joy rather than a bore. No, my love, it is Mrs. Mannering who has requested my company. It seems little Lucilla has the sense not to go."

"Then, why do you?"

Xanthe gave her that enigmatic smile. "Curiosity, I suppose. It shall be quite out of my ordinary experience. One can never tell what one might learn."

"Will you be back before the Denvilles' rout party?" she asked.

Titus, who had been sprawled on the bed, rolled to one side and emitted a short, staccato sound.

Xanthe laughed. "As he said, of course I shall. Now, how do you plan to spend the afternoon?"

"Addressing cards for our *soiree,* I suppose. And I shall invite Lucilla to drive with me in the park."

Xanthe beamed at her, and Phoebe found herself holding a bouquet of violets. "Have a delightful time, my dear." And with that, Xanthe hummed a bar, burst into a cascade of glittering particles and vanished.

Phoebe eyed the violets with uncertainty, glanced at Titus, who merely blinked at her, then sniffed the blossoms. Their sweet scent reassured her, so she carried them from the room to search out a bowl of water. Once she had them arranged, she scribbled a note to Lucy and dispatched it by the second footman.

The acceptance, coached in terms certain to make proud her former schoolmistress, came back less than ten minutes later. That left Phoebe with the remainder of the day, and mindful of her promise, she set to work on the invitation cards that had never seen the inside of a printer's shop. Why Xanthe hadn't bothered to add the directions of their guests, as well, Phoebe didn't quite understand, especially since this boring task fell to her. But since she never received straight answers from her godmother, she had long since given up asking the whys and wherefores of magic.

She had returned to the spacious apartment at the back of the house that served as a library, where she wrote a letter to Thomas while Titus sprawled in a patch of sunlight on the carpet, when the door opened and Arthur, the senior footman, showed Miles into the room. The force of his rage hit her even before she read it in his lowered brow and tightened jaw. She came to her feet and stood facing him, her hands clasping the back of her chair.

"I hope you are satisfied with what you have done," he declared through clenched teeth.

"What has happened?" she demanded, going straight for the important issue.

"Lucy has eloped with her damned fortune hunter!"

Phoebe opened her mouth to tell him it was absurd, but held her tongue. After a moment, she asked, "Did she leave you a note?"

"There was no need. She has vanished, along with her maid and a couple of bandboxes. They must be away to Gretna, and now you may see where your meddling has gotten us."

Ten

For a long moment, Miles glared at Phoebe. He didn't know why he had come here, he realized. Not to blame her; that did no good at this point. The possibility that he needed her support he rejected utterly. He simply wasted precious time. He turned on his heel and strode toward the door, his steps short, controlled, angry.

"Where are you going?" she demanded.

"After them. Where else?" he flung back at her.

"Wait!"

"Wait?" He spun about. "My dear girl—"

"You cannot go alone. Only consider. If you hope to bring her back—"

"I will," he broke in, grim.

"—with her reputation intact," Phoebe pursued, "then she must have some female companion to bear her countenance. Your aunt—"

"My aunt," he snapped, "is away from home. It was her intention not to return until this evening."

"Xanthe—" Phoebe began, then broke off. "Oh, bother, they have gone together, have they not."

"They have," Miles agreed. "Good God, are you all in league to ruin Lucy?"

"No one wants to ruin her," she flared back. "But if you had not practically forced her into Ashby's arms, this would never have happened."

"Forced her?" Miles glared at her. "I did no such thing. And if you will remember, I said not one word when she danced with that—" He broke off in time, recollecting that any epithet he might use to describe Lieutenant Gregory Harwich would not be fit for her ears. "Arguing will get us nowhere," he said through clenched teeth.

"At least we are in agreement about that," came her prompt response.

He nodded. "Since neither my aunt nor your godmother are available, you will have to come with me."

"I?" Her eyes kindled. "But would that not be meddling?"

"If you had not meddled to begin with, this would not have happened!" The moment the words escaped his mouth, he regretted them—and knew them to be untrue. "Miss Caldicot," he began stiffly, "that was unforgivable of me."

Her color, which had blanched at his first words, returned with vehemence. "We are both distressed over Lucy. We must concentrate on her, not on our differences. Of course I will go with you."

Relief flooded through him. "There are a few things I must take care of, then. I will return for you within the hour. Can you be ready?"

"I could leave now, if you wished it."

No missishness, no uncertainties. Her no-nonsense

approach relieved him. "I first need to discover when and how they have set forth. To dash off in mad pursuit, without an inkling of where they might change horses, would be foolish in the extreme." And with that, he left.

An hour didn't give him much time, he reflected as he strode out the door. If his groom would only hurry— The man did. Within minutes, Miles spotted his great roan turning the corner, the groom on his back. Another minute to lengthen the stirrups, and he swung onto Cuthbert's saddle. "Have the curricle here within the hour," he called over his shoulder, and set off at a brisk trot.

There were any number of hostelries and inns where one might hire a post chaise. Finding the right one would take time. He tried to consider what little he knew of Harwich, and came up with few facts. The man had precious little money, and he had need of secrecy. That probably eliminated the more reputable of the establishments. Which still left him with far too vast a number he would have to visit. He would begin, he decided, at those nearest the outskirts of town near the Great North Road.

He drew a blank at the first two at which he called. At the third, though, one of the ostlers remembered a young military cove, but they hadn't been able to accommodate him. "Try the Swan," the ostler suggested. "That's what I told 'im."

A half crown changed hands, and Miles rode to the stableyard of the inn less than two hundred yards along the street. Here, to his satisfaction, not only the ostlers, but the innkeeper himself, remembered Harwich as an engaging young man bent on escorting his sister back home to Yorkshire. The chaise had been hired for an indefinite period of time, but the postilions, along with only a single pair, his informants disclosed, had been hired for St. Albans, the Swan's usual first stage for such a journey.

"Brought the young lady here in a hackney," said the innkeeper, "then bundled her into the chaise and off they went. Oh, not 'til late in the day, it was. Going on a quarter past noon, wasn't it?" He turned to his head ostler for confirmation.

The man leaned on his shovel, gave the matter serious consideration, then nodded. "That's right. 'Twas just after twelve, it was."

Which put them barely three hours ahead, Miles reflected. His own bays could make far greater speed than a pair of job horses. He tried to calculate how far they might get, then gave up the effort as a waste of time. Only as far as St. Albans on their first stage, yet he felt certain they would not stop for the night so close to town. Harwich must be well aware of the inadequacies of hired cattle. He would change often. And that meant Miles would have word at that first posting house of when they left, how far they would go, and when he might hope to overtake them. That they headed for Gretna he had not a single doubt. Marriage had to be the purpose, for that was the only way Harwich could lay his hands on Lucy's considerable portion.

He returned to Half Moon Street only a little over an hour after he left. And there, pacing briskly toward him, came his bays, harnessed and fresh for the trip.

Miles jumped from his saddle; but before he could mount the steps to Phoebe's house, her door opened, and she appeared, carrying a pelisse, a lap robe, and a hamper. She looked fresh and poised, a bright smile on her face as if they embarked upon a pleasure expedition.

She greeted him gaily, extending her hand. "How charming of you to be punctual," she said in a voice calculated to reach the footman who had followed her from the house, carrying a satchel. An oddly familiar satchel—his own, in fact. "It is so very kind of you to take me to my godmother. James," she added, turning to the footman, "I forgot to tell Cook we shall not be in for dinner. And if Lady Xanthe is tired, we might remain the night." She gave the man a dazzling smile, then accepted Miles's aid in climbing into the carriage. Miles stowed her various parcels, sent his groom off with Cuthbert to convey a message to his aunt and Lady Xanthe, then gave the bays the office and started for the Great North Road.

"I had your man pack a few things for you," she said as they turned the corner. "I hope you do not mind."

"On the contrary. You seem to have shown amazing foresight. Had I been thinking clearly, I should have done so myself, and suggested you do the same. I am in your debt. How, by the way, did you fob off poor Vines?"

Her lips twitched. "I had only to tell him that you were taking me to Miss Lucy, and he could not have been more helpful."

Miles gave a short nod. "Did he suspect the truth?"

"I tried to come up with a convincing story of your aunt taking ill." She sighed. "I fear I have been telling a great many lies."

He spared her a quick glance. "You do not sound penitent."

"No. Quite shocking, is it not? What did you discover?"

He told her, and she listened, not interrupting with unnecessary questions. "And what the deuce I'm to do with her now—" He broke off, and he forced his fingers to unclench from the reins.

"There is no harm in her," Phoebe said with surprising gentleness. "She is simply strong-willed, and trying to find her feet."

"No easy task, I suppose, when she is under the guardianship of someone else who is not only strong-willed, but far too accustomed to having his own way." When she made no response to this gambit, he cast her a sideways glance. "What, showing restraint? This is a new comeout for you."

She shook her head, smiling. "The urge was almost irresistible, too. But now isn't the time for us to argue."

"True," he agreed. "There will be plenty of time for that once we have Lucy safe again." He felt her hand on his arm, a fleeting touch of comfort and encouragement. It warmed him.

"We will have her safe," she said, and it came out as a promise. "I cannot believe Xanthe would have left town if anything of a serious nature were to happen."

He wished he could share her confidence; then the

oddness of that last statement struck him. He pondered her meaning until they reached the outskirts of town, at which point his reflections returned once more to finding Lucy and dealing with that scoundrel Harwich. Phoebe sat in silence at his side, not interrupting his murderous thoughts. As they escaped the heavier traffic and he sprang his horses, urging them to show their speed, her only response was to put one hand up to hold her bonnet.

As the miles slipped past, he began to consider the road ahead. Harwich's equipage was scheduled to make its first change at the White Hart, just outside St. Albans. He had best do the same; he had pressed his bays sadly to gain what time he could. He could only hope the post boys at the White Hart would have an accustomed stopping place for the end of their stage. Knowing the expected destinations would make tracing the couple that much easier.

He drove on, his thoughts focused on the enquiries he must make at the inn, the chances of finding suitable cattle capable of carrying him with the necessary speed for the next step of this wild journey. He must have gained time on them; how much, though, he had no idea. Probably not enough.

The sun had advanced far in the western sky when they at last reached the town, swept through it, and continued along the road until the posting inn came into sight. This proved to be a medium-sized establishment of a design that dated no farther back than the reign of the first King George. The yard, though not spacious according to the standards of most posting houses, boasted sufficient stabling to supply more horses than seemed likely would be needed at one of the less-frequented stops. Miles looped his rein, turned smartly through the gate, then drew in his bays at sight of the post-chaise and pair that stood waiting in the care of two post boys and an ostler. A small hand grasped his forearm. He glanced down to see Phoebe sitting erect, her bright eyes wide.

"It couldn't possibly be them, could it?" she breathed.

He drew his horses to a halt, then fleetingly covered her fingers with his own. "It doesn't seem likely." Yet he could not quell the surge of hope that rushed through him.

A second ostler emerged from the stables and ran to the bays' heads, looking up expectantly for instructions. Miles swung down, patted a sweat-streaked flank on the near horse, and addressed the wiry little man who faced him. "Whose carriage is that?"

A frown of concentration creased the man's brow. "Military gent, sir," he said after a moment.

"Is it, indeed." A slow, satisfied smile tugged at the corners of Miles's mouth. He turned back to the curricle and reached up to help Phoebe to alight. "It seems it is possible," he informed her.

She clasped his hand that held hers. "Do you wish me to wait out here?"

"Do you trust me not to terrify Lucilla?" came his prompt response. He felt oddly elated, as if a great weight of worry had lifted from him. He helped Phoebe down, then tucked her hand through his arm and led the way toward the stately front of the inn.

They stepped into darkness from the late afternoon

light, and it took a moment for his eyes to adjust. They stood in an entry hall that smelled of vinegar and lemon oil. From somewhere down the narrow hall stretching before them came the distinct odor of frying onions. To the left an open doorway led into a common room, and by the waning sunlight that drifted through the windows Miles could make out the shapes of three patrons seated at one of the trestle tables at the far side of the room. To the right lay a closed door and a narrow staircase of pale oak leading upwards to where the murmur of angry voices could be heard.

Miles put his hand on the banister, but before he could mount more than three steps, a middle-aged woman of comfortable proportions, garbed in a gray stuff gown, apron and mobcap, hurried down the hall to greet them. She bore all the appearance of one who had not had an easy day. "Would you be liking a glass of wine or a mug of ale, sir? Ma'am?" She looked from Miles to Phoebe, then back again. "I'm very much afraid the private parlor's bespoke; but the taproom is near empty, and the young lady and her brother should be off at any moment." She cast an uneasy glance up the stairs.

"A young lady and her brother, is it?" Miles smiled at her. "And her brother is a military gentleman?"

The woman blinked at him. "Why, however did you know, sir?"

"I am somewhat acquainted with them. They will have no objection to our sharing their parlor."

"Well, now." The woman smiled in patent relief. "That is a good thing, then. I didn't quite like showing your good lady into a common room, that I didn't.

But you'll be quite comfortable in our parlor, and the young lady doesn't seem to be coming down yet."

At that moment, a young female voice rose on a wail. "I won't come out, and there is nothing you can do to make me! You are not my brother, and I don't know how they can believe such odious lies!"

Miles's eyebrows rose. "There seems to be an altercation."

The woman lowered her voice, even though there was no chance it would carry to the combatants above stairs. "Miss does not want to return to her guardian's home, poor dear."

The sympathy, to Miles's ear, sounded spurious. He stiffened. "That, I take it, is what the gentleman says. And what does the young lady say?"

The woman cast a worried glance up the steps. "Well, as to that, she came out with some farfetched story of being an heiress, and the gentleman abducting her, and she has bolted herself into our best front bedchamber and refuses to come out."

"Has she, by God." He glanced down at Phoebe, and read the mixture of relief and amusement on her face.

"She always was resourceful," Phoebe murmured.

He nodded. "And as for Harwich—" He mounted the stairs.

The innkeeper, a chambermaid, and a soldier in scarlet regimentals stood in the hall outside a closed door. The soldier leaned low, addressing the keyhole in cajoling tones, while the other two stood just behind him, the maid watching with avid interest, the innkeeper with a harassed frown. Miles strolled forward, coming to a stop about a yard away. He watched for a moment, then said, in a carefully casual voice, "Having a problem, Harwich?"

The effect on the lieutenant was all Miles could have hoped for. First the man went rigid; then he straightened slowly and turned to face Miles, the color draining from his face.

"Just so," said Miles.

"I—" Harwich broke off, and a ghastly smile spread across his face. "This is not—"

"I know perfectly well what this is," said Miles, and gave vent to his pent-up sentiments by planting the lieutenant a facer that leveled him.

The chambermaid screamed. The innkeeper started forward only to stop again almost at once. Miles stood over his victim, rubbing the knuckles of his right hand, feeling for once completely satisfied. Harwich struggled up to one elbow, then remained there, shaking his head slowly, his fingers probing his bloodied nose.

Miles stepped over him, taking his place at the door. "Lucy?" he called. "You can come out now."

A moment's silence followed. Then, "Miles?" Her tone wavered on a note of hysteria. "Miles?" she repeated, and there came a sound of scraping, as of some heavy piece of furniture being dragged across the floorboards.

"Efficient," commented Phoebe.

Miles glanced over his shoulder to where she stood, eyeing the scene with obvious enjoyment. He raised his eyebrows. "You approve?"

"Far better than pistols at dawn. That would undoubtedly create exactly the sort of scandal you most want to avoid."

"Sir—" The innkeeper pushed forward, his expression one of consternation. "The gentleman—"

"The gentleman," said Miles, turning the word into a sneer, "has abducted the lady, just as she tried to tell you."

"But—" The man paled.

A final scraping screech sounded from within; then a bolt rattled, and Lucy dragged open the door, stumbled forward, and flung herself into Miles's arms. He held her a moment, then set her aside. "Really, my dear. Have a care for my coat."

"Oh, Miles—" Lucy started to laugh, but it broke on a sob. Then her brimming eyes widened. "Miss Caldicot!" she wailed, and flung herself upon her new victim. "Oh, Miss Caldicot, it has been dreadful! He—he abducted me."

"Yes, to be sure," said Phoebe. She looked up. "Wine, to your private parlor, I believe," she said to the innkeeper. "Sir Miles, will you help me take her down?"

Miles came to Lucy's side, and in spite of the brave tilt to her head, he found he had to support her trembling steps as they descended to the privacy of the room on the ground floor. Once inside, he half carried her to a settle before the hearth, and she sank onto it, shuddering. For several minutes she sat in silence, with Phoebe beside her, holding her hand, until the door opened to admit not the innkeeper, but his wife, bearing a bottle of wine and three glasses. She cast an uneasy glance over the group, laid down her burden, and left the room.

Miles poured the wine—canary, he saw with approval—and pressed a glass into his sister's hand. "How came this about, Lucy?"

She sniffed. "I never went with him on purpose!" she declared.

"No," he soothed. "Of course you did not."

"You don't believe me! But Miles, truly, I told him this morning I could not consent to an elopement, even though he made it sound like the most romantic of adventures, but truly, I—I had begun to suspect I might not like to have him as a husband after all."

"And how did he take that?" Though Miles thought he could guess.

She took another sip of her wine. "He said he should not press me, that he should never wish to cause me distress, and that he should always stand my friend." Her eyes gleamed, and she gave a short, shaky laugh. "And I was fool enough to believe him. I did not see him again until just before noon, when he came to the house and told me Wicken—my maid, you know," she explained to Phoebe, "—he said Wicken had hurt her ankle, and would I come and help him bring her home. And—and I did, only we went to this horrid inn, and before I knew what he was about, he pushed me into a post chaise and jumped in after me, and he—he threatened to gag me if I tried to scream." Her eyes kindled. "I did anyway, and he clamped his hand over my mouth, so I bit him."

"Brava," Miles murmured.

She sniffed. "Yes, but then he cursed at me and

stuffed a handkerchief in my mouth, and tied another about my head, and said he should keep it there until I promised not to make a fuss, and that it would be a very long and uncomfortable trip to Scotland if I did not behave exactly as he said I must."

"My poor dear." Phoebe stroked back Lucy's hair.

"So what did you do?" Miles regarded his sister with fascination.

"I pretended to be afraid, and agreed to whatever he said. And then," she added on a note of triumph, "I pretended to become sick with the motion of the carriage. He looked quite apprehensive, too," she added with a note of satisfaction. "When we stopped here, I begged for the chance to lie down for a moment, and asked for a burnt feather and a vinaigrette, and then I locked myself into the room. Only that foolish landlord believed Gregory's ridiculous story about my running away from my supposed guardian, and I think if you had not come, they would have carried out their threat of taking the door apart to get me out. Gregory even promised to take me back to London if I insisted, but I didn't believe him."

From outside came the sounds of horses' hooves and the crunch of carriage wheels on gravel. Miles stiffened. "Harwich," he breathed. In one movement he was on his feet and out the door. Behind him, he heard Phoebe call out to leave Harwich be, but that was the one thing Miles could not do. Not that he planned anything dramatic, such as beating the man to within an inch of his life, or—to be even more melodramatic—challenge him to a duel. He merely wished to assure himself that the lieutenant kept the events of this day to himself, and did not seek to repeat them with any other innocent young lady. It shouldn't be too hard to convince Harwich not to show his face again in London. It would, after all, be a very bruised face for some time to come, when he finished with it. His hands clenched into punishing bunches of fives as he allowed this pleasant thought to take up residence in his mind. He intended to enjoy, with extreme satisfaction, the next several minutes.

He emerged into the gathering dusk in time to see Harwich clambering hastily into the carriage. Miles strode forward, catching his arm before the man could swing the door closed behind himself. He jerked the lieutenant about, observing with grim satisfaction the look of terror on the man's face. "I believe we have some unsettled business," Miles said in a purely conversational tone. His grip tightened as the chaise swayed to the uneasy sidlings of the pair harnessed to the traces.

"Let go of me!" breathed Harwich. His countenance had paled, but a tightness set in about his jaw. "Or I'll shoot," he added, his voice cracking.

Miles glanced down to see a pistol clutched in the man's right hand. It lurched out to steady him against the doorframe as the body of the chaise swayed again.

"I mean it," Harwich added, regaining his footing and leveling the pistol at Miles's chest.

"Don't be a fool." Miles grabbed the barrel of the gun, pushing it away.

The off horse backed, sending the chaise off on another unsteady swing, and Harwich lost his balance. He fell, and the pistol went off as his arm jerked outward to catch himself. The explosion rang in Miles's ears, deafening him to all else.

Then he became aware of warmth traveling down his arm, followed by a stab of fire and the acrid scent of burned cloth. He stared at his shoulder, where the ball had ripped through his coat and into his flesh, and watched the blood flow down his arm, turning the blue of his coat to a deep purple. He looked back at Harwich and saw the man staring at him in horror. Their eyes met, Miles smiled, and for the second time that afternoon he knocked the lieutenant down.

Eleven

The next few minutes passed in a blur for Miles. A great deal of blood seemed to be flowing through the fingers he clamped over his shoulder. Ostlers came at a run, the front door of the inn banged open and the pounding of innumerable feet reached him. And Harwich—Miles looked up to see the lieutenant thrusting the coachman from his box and scrambling into his place. The postilion, who had not yet mounted, jumped back as the horses sprang forward under Harwich's agitated command.

"Miles!" Lucilla ran toward him, and was only prevented from throwing herself against his chest by Phoebe's prompt action.

That inestimable young woman grabbed his sister, holding her back. "You will get blood all over your gown," she said with what, to Miles, seemed like eminent good sense.

The chaise careened out the gate, scraping along one side. The near leader, deprived of a controlling postilion, reared, sending the vehicle skidding sideways. For a moment the carriage teetered on its two off wheels; then it overset, sending Harwich flying into the dirt. The postilion and ostlers sprang forward to tend the frightened horses.

"Do you suppose they will think to detain Harwich?" Miles asked Phoebe. She stood at his side, pressing a folded towel against his shoulder. It hurt abominably.

"I have told the innkeeper to see to it. I have also instructed one of the ostlers to ride for a doctor, and it is possible he will remember in the near future."

He eyed her with a mixture of approval and annoyance. "You have everything under control, it would seem."

"Not the bleeding, I fear," and her note of cheerfulness sounded a bit forced. "Lucy." She turned to his sister, who stood with her hands to her cheeks; her face, down which silent tears slipped, looked unnaturally pale. "Will you oblige me by dealing with our good landlord's wife? I requested her to take hot water, towels, and a basin to the parlor, but she seems to be unable to move from the front door. Do hurry, my dear. I wish to get your brother inside so we can take his coat off."

"I can take off my own coat," he protested. "And I can hold that damned pad for myself." He clamped his hand over it.

Phoebe stood back. "Landlord?" She looked to where he stood, hands clasping his apron, watching the activity just outside his gate. "Brandy, if you please. Will it take the doctor long to get here?"

"What?" He turned his appalled gaze on them. "Begging your pardon, miss. No, it won't take long. And brandy. Of course. At once, miss. To think of such a thing happening here." He hurried off, disappearing into the dark interior of his establishment.

Phoebe returned her attention to Miles. "Let us get you inside."

"Do you intend to carry me?" he demanded. "I am able to get myself within." He started forward, and a wave of dizziness from loss of blood set his next step staggering.

She caught his arm, steadying him, and for a moment he leaned on her. Then the light-headedness passed, and the burning pain of his wound took over. A shot or two of brandy sounded like an excellent plan. He strode forward, gritting his teeth to keep from crying out.

Lucy emerged from the inn, running to his side, her eyes wide and frightened. "Oh, Miles, I am so terribly sorry." The tears brimmed, threatening to overflow once more.

He didn't feel up to dealing with an hysterical little sister, but he would have to try. Yet before he could speak, Phoebe said, "Pillows! Lucy, my dear, will you run back in and request extra pillows? And a blanket. We must keep your brother comfortable until the doctor arrives. No," she added as the girl protested. "I will stay with him. Hurry, please. And you," she added to Miles, "need not walk so quickly, if you please. You will only increase the bleeding."

From behind them came the sounds of the horses being led back and the voices of the men arguing about the best method of righting the chaise. What had become of Harwich, Miles found he didn't particularly care. Right now, all he really wanted to do was sit down for a minute or two, then escort Lucy safely back to town.

They entered the inn, and it wasn't until Phoebe guided him toward the private parlor that he realized he still leaned on her arm. He straightened, and that irritating dizziness washed over him once more. She steered him safely inside, then pressed him onto a chair. He leaned back against a pillow that his sister pushed quickly into place. "You are both making a great deal of fuss over the most trifling scratch," he protested.

"Of course we are," soothed Phoebe, and pressed a glass into his hand. "Drink this." He did, and the amber liquid burned down his throat, sending fire through him, strengthening his weakened muscles. His foggy head cleared, and the pain in his shoulder became more vivid.

"Over there, Mrs. Beechum, thank you," said Phoebe's soft voice.

He realized he'd closed his eyes, and opened them to see the innkeeper's wife placing a basin of steaming water on a table. A chambermaid hovered in her wake, her arms loaded with towels and strips of linen.

Phoebe turned back to him. "I believe it will be best if we cut your coat off."

"You do, do you?" He eyed her with disapproval. "I am perfectly capable of taking it off."

"Of course you are." A sudden smile, albeit a wan one, lit her lovely eyes. "But this is *my* turn to be managing, and I will not let you spoil it for me." She took the scissors held out to her by Mrs. Beechum and set to work on the sleeve.

Her hair smelled of violets, he noted as she leaned close, intent on her work. It reminded him of the night they had visited the Pershings. Only then he had been rescuing her. And now—

He winced, fighting back an involuntary cry as she sliced the fabric away from his wound. *Damn* that scoundrel! He drew a steadying breath, and found she leaned over him, this time holding out his refilled glass.

"I am sorry," she said. She had finished with the coat; at least she had cut through the sleeve and across the breast, pulling it back to reveal the slashed and bloodied remnants of his fine linen shirt. She now set to work on this, cutting away the fabric until the ugly, jagged wound lay revealed.

"Basilicum powder," he muttered, and was annoyed that his voice sounded hazy, as if a mere two brandies had left him cup shot.

"We need to remove the torn fibers of your shirt, first," she said, and reached for a cloth that had been soaking in the hot water.

He turned his head away and studied the fire that someone had lit in the grate. Lucy sat near it, her hands clasped in her lap, her wide-eyed gaze resting on him. He managed a smile for her that won no response. "It's not as bad as all that, my girl," he said, forcing a joking note into his voice. He winced at Phoebe's gentle proddings, annoyed with himself that he had not been able to control the reaction.

Lucy sniffed. "It is bleeding terribly!" she wailed.

"What, still?" he demanded in a feeble attempt at mock alarm. "Miss Caldicot, I must protest."

"It is only from the washing, Lucy," that lady said in a voice tinged with forced amusement. "Once it is clean, we may put pressure on it again. If you like, you may hold the bandage this time."

Miles glared at her. "I do not need anyone to hold anything."

"To be sure you do not," she said, quite affably. "But have a consideration for your poor sister, who must sit there doing nothing. It is a terrible strain on one's nerves."

"Hers or mine?" he murmured.

Phoebe's lips twitched. "There, you are more yourself now. I shall shortly expect you to start countermanding my every instruction."

"My dear Miss Caldicot," he said, his own smile somewhat wry, "I would not dare."

The doctor arrived a very few minutes later, and after a thorough inspection of Phoebe's handiwork, which caused Miles's teeth to clench and the perspiration to stand out on his brow, was pleased to approve her efforts. He dusted the torn flesh with basilicum powder, stitched the skin back together, then gave it one more dusting for good measure. This task complete, he wadded a pad of linen and strapped it into place with long strips that wound across his patient's body, strapping his upper left arm to his side. Phoebe watched the proceedings with no outward sign of consternation, except for a heightened color in her cheeks. Miles met her gaze and managed a smile for her, but she turned away.

The doctor pressed a glass in his hand. He swallowed a mouthful of the contents, realized it was not brandy, and glared at it with suspicion.

"Laudanum," the man said. "You'll be glad of it if you plan to return to London tonight as the lady says."

He shook his head. "Have to drive," he said.

A short laugh escaped the man. "Do you, now. With one hand? Best put up for the night here, though you'll find you'll not have the use of it yet tomorrow, either."

Miles leaned back in the chair, absently tossed off the rest of the contents, then abruptly realized what he had done and swore softly. The important thing at the moment was to see Lucy safe again at home, with no touch of scandal clinging to her name. How that was to be avoided, with him sporting an obvious injury, he did not know. In fact, he found it increasingly difficult to think with any clarity. Damned laudanum, it would probably put him to sleep if he weren't careful.

He forced his drooping lids open and reached out his good hand toward Phoebe, who had accompanied the departing doctor to the door. She returned to Miles's side, taking his hand in her own, and the coolness of her skin soothed him. "Got to keep this quiet," he said, and realized he mumbled.

"I've been thinking about that." She drew up a chair and settled at his side. "I believe we may count on Harwich to keep silent about his part in today's doings, out of fear of the law. Mr. Beechum—the landlord—is almost as anxious as we to avoid any scandal, especially after the shocking way he refused to listen to poor Lucy. He'll do his utmost to keep his people from talking, though a show of generosity on your part might help. As for your shoulder, and the fact Lucy or I shall be driving your curricle back into London, I believe we may best account for that with a tale of our being overturned."

He eyed her with disapprobation. "No one who knows me would believe that for a moment."

"Do you prefer highwaymen?" she inquired sweetly.

He closed his eyes. "Oh, go to the devil," he muttered, and allowed the fuzzy darkness to envelope him.

Phoebe sat in the chair, still holding Miles's hand, feeling the solid bones, the strength of it even though he slept. Mostly, her thoughts dwelled on the sight of his muscled chest, with its thick covering of curling dark hair. Her cheeks warmed once more, and she couldn't keep her gaze from resting on him, where the linen bandages crisscrossed his torso. She wanted to touch him, and the mere prospect left her breathless.

And as for the impropriety of her longings—

Resolutely she turned from him, found the blanket Lucy had fetched, and draped it over him. He looked so peaceful, with the pain and strain released from his face. She touched his cheek, feeling the roughness of the beard that had not been scraped away since that morning. The scent of old leather and bay rum clung to him, evoking images of moonlight and gardens, of chandeliers and soft music and a country dance.

Her palm found his and pressed against it; then her fingers closed about his. Did all the caring lie on her side? A couple of times she had thought—she had hoped—he might feel something for her, something not induced by Xanthe's magic, something more than acceptance, tolerance, liking. Friendship could be a wonderful thing. But even that was but a pale shadow of what she now knew she longed for from him.

The door opened, and with a last, lingering caress, she released his hand. "Is all ready, Lucy?" she asked as the girl came in. "Then, let us see him safely to a bedchamber."

Lucy eyed her brother with uncertainty. "He will be very angry with us."

Phoebe shook her head. "Only because he did not have the ordering of it all. He will be better for the rest, and glad that you have been returned to London with complete propriety. We shall send his man to him as soon as we get back, and we may drive out to visit him tomorrow. When he has returned to his senses, he will see that this is the best course."

She didn't want to leave him. Every instinct told her to stay, to care for him. But she had to see to Lucy, first. He would be all right here, she assured herself. Yet even after he had been moved to a bedchamber and tucked between sheets, she lingered at his side. Not even the promises of Mrs. Beechum to sit with him until Vines should arrive eased her distress. She wanted to be at his side, though she knew there was nothing she could do that the comfortable innkeeper's wife could not do just as well. At last, forced by the lateness of the hour, she ushered Lucy down to the chaise that had been righted and readied, and they embarked for London.

Lucy sat in silence for a very long time, staring out into the darkness of the evening, until a shaky sob escaped her. "It should have been the other way around," she wailed. "I quite wanted Miles to run him through with a sword, or put a bullet into him. It should not have been Miles who was hurt. Oh, Miss Caldicot, I feel so dreadful about that."

"He won't blame you," Phoebe said with certainty.

"I know." Lucy sniffed, seeking her handkerchief in her reticule. "But I would much rather he ranted and railed at me. I feel so guilty."

The terrors and exhaustion of the day finally took their toll, and Lucy drifted off into an uneasy doze. Phoebe stared into the gathering night, her thoughts far from her surroundings. The shadowy shapes of trees and hedges faded into a remembered vision of Miles, slumped back in his chair, eyes closed, a lock of dark hair falling forward over his forehead, his chest bare except for the bandages. Thoughts like that would never do, she chided herself. With a sigh she sank back into her corner, and her tired, wayward mind once more returned to Miles.

They arrived in Half Moon Street shortly after nine that night to find both Mrs. Mannering and Xanthe in the former's house, engaged upon a game of cards. Mrs. Mannering laid these aside as they entered the room, but she displayed none of the signs of a doting aunt in the throes of anxiety over the well being of her charges. She enveloped Lucy in an embrace, listened to Phoebe's explanations with only a few cries of dismay, and sighed at the completion of the narrative.

"You were quite right," she said to Xanthe with a rueful smile. "They were perfectly capable of handling matters on their own. But poor Miles." She shook her head. "I suppose I cannot be seen to race to his side, but Vines shall depart at once."

It actually took half an hour for that devoted servitor to pack into two valises extra bandages, salves, balms, and every other item he felt necessary for his master's comfort and well-being, and depart to take up his vigil. In the meantime, the others were not idle. Even before Vines set forth in the hired chaise that had been fitted with new horses, Phoebe and Lucy found themselves hustled into evening gowns by their respective chaperons, then into Xanthe's barouche for the short drive to Lady Denville's rout party.

They were not even late, Phoebe reflected as they mounted the steps to their hostess's drawing rooms. They had a ready explanation of Miles's having received an urgent summons to return to his estates, and Lucy blithely assured all inquirers that she expected him back in town within a day or two. Phoebe watched the girl with growing pride; with all the cause in the world to indulge in a fit of the vapors, still Lucy conducted herself with admirable control. A haunted look might linger in her glittering eyes, and her laugh might sound brittle, but no one could guess that within the preceding eight hours she had been abducted and seen her brother shot.

At her side, Lucy emitted a soft "oh!" Phoebe turned in time to see Ashby standing in the doorway, his gaze scanning the room. The next moment he set forth to greet his hostess. Lucy started forward after him, then checked herself and cast an apologetic glance toward Phoebe. With a slight gesture of her head, Phoebe brought Lucy back to where Mrs. Mannering sat in a corner beside a potted palm, deep in conversation with a frail, elderly woman who bore all the appearance of an impoverished relative elevated to the role of chaperon.

Lucy took a chair at her aunt's side, but her gaze returned to Ashby. That gentleman, having paid his respects, turned to survey the room through his quizzing glass. His gaze fell on Lucy, and he allowed his glass to drop as he strolled toward her, pausing only to greet his numerous acquaintances. Within a few minutes he was bowing before Mrs. Mannering, then turning to take Lucy's hand. A slight crease formed in his brow. "What's toward, m'girl?"

She returned the pressure of his fingers. "Oh, Simon, how very glad I am to see you." Her voice, so strictly controlled until now, trembled.

An arrested expression flickered in his eyes, and very slowly, his gaze still holding hers, he raised the hand he still clasped to his lips. Her eyes widened, and for a very long moment she simply stared at him. Smiling down at her, he seated himself at her side. "You may tell me about it presently, when there aren't so many people around," he said softly, then embarked on one of his amusing tales about his cousin's litter of puppies, now eight weeks old.

To Phoebe's satisfaction, the haggard lines faded from around Lucy's eyes. Now, if only Miles were here, to soothe her own troubled spirits. But then, if he were here, and uninjured, she would not be suffering such distress.

She strolled away to exchange greetings with the elderly General Fotheringham, then drifted off to stand with two other young ladies. Lucy, she noted, had accompanied Ashby to the refreshments table, and they conversed with Lady Maria Sparling and her son, Viscount Dreydon. Lucy's reputation, she reflected, was safe. After an hour of thus mingling with their fellow guests, no one would ever believe that anything untoward had occurred that day. Lucy derived strength and comfort from Ashby, and he—Phoebe smiled—he basked in this unaccustomed role of Lucy's chosen supporter.

She detached herself from her companions and moved on to join another group. What she really wanted to do, of course, was to go home. No, that wasn't true. She wanted to return to the inn and sit by Miles's bedside, tend to him, reassure herself he would be all right. But she couldn't do that. All she could do for him at the moment was stand by his sister.

At last, they made their excuses and headed home. By then, the shocks of the day had begun to wear off, and it occurred to Phoebe that she wanted a word in private with her godmother. Not until after they had seen Lucy and Mrs. Mannering into their house, though, and had entered their own home, could Phoebe hope for the chance. As soon as the maid who waited on her had finished preparing her for bed, Phoebe slipped out of her room and across the hall, where she rapped with impatient knuckles on Xanthe's door. It opened of its own volition, allowing Phoebe to step inside.

At first glance, the room appeared empty. Suspicious, Phoebe peered about for some sign of her unpredictable fairy godmother, but saw only Titus sprawled across the bed, bathing his large expanse of stomach. "Where is she?" she demanded of the feline.

Titus paused in his ablutions, blinked at her, emitted a short "myap" sound, and looked in the direction of the candle that burned bright on the dressing table.

The glow expanded, haloing outward in an ever increasing circle, then began to take on a vaguely human form. Phoebe watched, her arms folded before her, not in the mood to be impressed. Luminescent wings took shape, and a single gold-tipped feather drifted to the floor. Xanthe stood before her, eyebrows raised questioningly, amusement hovering about her mouth.

Phoebe waited several seconds longer, until Xanthe's display had come to an end, then said, "You went away on purpose today, and took Mrs. Mannering with you!"

The wings closed, then opened once more, and a puzzled expression entered Xanthe's luminous eyes. "Of course I did, my love. Did you not guess it from the start?"

"How *could* you? Had you no thought for what might have happened to Lucy?"

"I had every thought for it. As well as to what might happen to you."

"And to Sir Miles?" This Phoebe said through clenched teeth. "Madam, he was shot!"

Xanthe nodded. "But not injured severely. No, I believe everything progresses quite well."

"Well? Do you mean to tell me you *intended* all this to happen?"

"Not in the least. My dear, I had nothing to do with

Lucilla's abduction. I merely refrained from interfering with it. As I have told you before, I do not control outcomes, I merely provide opportunities. Each of you chose how you would behave today. And I must say, you all handled it extremely well."

"And what if Lucy had been harmed?" she demanded.

At that, a tinge of guilt crept over Xanthe's expression. "I did bend my rules a little," she admitted. "Lucy was safe from any harm the entire time."

"But not Miles!"

"No," she agreed. "Not Sir Miles. He, like you, must make his own choices."

Phoebe considered that for a moment. "And what happens now?"

"Now?" Xanthe gave her that infuriatingly enigmatic smile. "Now we wait and see."

Wait proved the apt word. Mrs. Mannering and Lucy made the journey to visit Miles the following morning, escorted by Lord Ashby. Phoebe did not. Listless, she accompanied her godmother on a round of morning visits, then settled in the library to read a book that totally failed to hold her attention. She kept looking at the clock, knowing that did no good. They would probably remain with him for the entire day, and not return until evening. But just after she had gone upstairs to change into a carriage dress for the afternoon Promenade in the park, Lucy arrived, breathless and happy, to inform her that her brother was once more safe beneath their own roof.

"I cannot but be glad," the girl said, "but he is so

dreadfully pale, I do wish he had remained another day at the inn."

"Could you not have prevailed upon him?" Phoebe exclaimed, though she knew his stubbornness well enough to know that once he had made up his mind, there would be no swaying him.

"We had not the chance," Lucy explained, "for we met him on the road, less than five miles from London, too. And he was as sulky as a bear because he could not drive his own pair, and he says that Vines is heavy-handed. He was quite out of temper, and most uncivil when I suggested that I might drive his curricle for him. He actually accused me of being likely to overturn him in a ditch, as if I could be so cowhanded! And he would not enter Aunt Jane's chaise, even though we told him he should be ever so much more comfortable in it. So Simon drove him."

"I am sure he much preferred it that way. Is—is he very cross with me?"

Lucy cast her a glance from beneath her lashes. "He was pleased to hear we had attended the rout party last night."

But not, Phoebe wagered, that they had left him at the inn. She smoothed the wrinkle her fingers had creased in her skirt and said, in an off-hand manner, "Is he up to receiving visitors?"

Lucy eyed her dubiously. "The doctor has given him more laudanum, though there was quite an argument over his taking it. He did charge me with a message for you, though. He says he shall pay you a morning visit on the morrow."

It was on the tip of her tongue to ask whether he

would be up to dressing and paying a formal call, but she bit it back. He would do precisely as he wished, no matter what she said. Which left her only to await what she suspected would be an uncomfortable and highly formal interview the next day.

She was right. He arrived punctually as the clock struck ten, dressed with his usual elegant propriety, with only the slightest bulge about his left shoulder to indicate a bandage remained. He strode into the salon on the heels of the majordomo with all his usual athletic grace, and bowed over her hand with a reserved stiffness that owed nothing to any wounds. Phoebe expressed her pleasure at seeing him abroad and offered him a glass of wine.

This he refused with a curt word of thanks, then forged ahead with his purpose. "It seems I have much to thank you for, Miss Caldicot."

No warmth, no friendliness of a shared adventure, only the stiltedness of a deeply chagrined gentleman. The wound to his pride caused by her assuming control must be far more painful than the one to his shoulder. Somehow, she must cajole him down from his high ropes, restore him to his usual humorous outlook on events.

She offered her most conciliatory smile. "Not in the least. I am dreadfully sorry we were forced to leave you at the inn, but I knew you would understand the necessity of returning Lucy to town."

"I did. I find myself deeply in your debt. If you had not been with us to take charge of Lucy—"

"Well, I was," Phoebe broke in hastily, dismayed by his refusal to unbend. "So let us hear no more about it. It was my pleasure. I am well paid back by having been privileged to take part in the discomfiture of that rogue."

Miles bowed again, still not smiling. He renewed his thanks, then took his leave.

Phoebe, watching the stiff figure retreat through the door, suffered a lowering of her spirits. He might express undying gratitude, but she doubted he could forgive her for placing him so deeply in her debt. Or was it the fact she had managed all, without need of his aid, that weighed so heavily with him?

She did not see him for the remainder of the day, nor the morning of the next. That he might be keeping to his room seemed to her highly unlikely, which left her to suppose he avoided her company. She felt restless, and somewhat depressed. Her morning ride she took alone, and found much of the delight gone out of it, which depressed her even further. She wanted to see him again—and again, and again. It occurred to her she might just as well have done him a singular disservice; the result would have been very much the same.

When Lucy joined her for a drive in the park that afternoon, her first words dispelled the mystery and renewed Phoebe's alarm. "He left town this morning, heading for the Towers—our home in Surrey, you must know," that young lady declared.

Phoebe regarded her in no little alarm. "Surely he did not undertake such a journey with that injured arm! He could not possibly drive."

"Mr. Dauntry took him in his tilbury, since Simon did not wish to leave town at present." A soft flush crept into the girl's cheeks, and she hurried on. "I am in the greatest quake what might have taken him down there."

"Is there trouble on the estate?" Phoebe asked with polite concern, though her worry lay more in the harm the journey might have done Miles.

Lucy wrinkled her nose. "There is nothing amiss at all. He was restless all day yesterday, and we feared— Aunt Jane and I—that he would bring on a fever; but at last he seemed to come to some decision and went off to see Simon, and then Mr. Dauntry."

"He probably needed to manage something," Phoebe said, striving for a light note. And what she said was probably true. He would work on the estate, make some decisions, regain his sense of being in control, and return to town restored to his usual confidence.

It was Phoebe who suffered. Every day he remained away seemed an eternity to her, for they had parted on indifferent terms. She needed to see him, see the warm smile light his eyes once more as his gaze rested on her. His continued absence quite cut up her peace.

The morning of the fifth day after his departure brought Lucy to her doorstep. Phoebe sat in the morning room, going over the menu for their small dinner party that night, when Alfred announced Miss Saunderton and ushered the girl into the room. Phoebe laid down her pen, and Lucy came forward a few steps, regarding Phoebe with wide, considering eyes. Phoebe greeted her, both curious and amused by the girl's odd manner.

As soon as they were seated opposite one another

in the comfortable chairs, Lucy came directly to the point. "Have you seen my brother since he returned to town yesterday?"

"Yesterday?" A hollowness yawned in Phoebe's stomach. "No. Did he—is he quite recovered? No ill effects from the journey?"

Lucy eyed Phoebe with perturbation. "He seemed terribly preoccupied. And he did not call upon you at once. Oh, this is dreadful."

"What is?" Phoebe fought her sense of unease. "Surely your brother could not be about anything so terrible as all that. It is hardly in his nature."

"But it is!" Lucy declared with considerable heat. "You know how much he likes to have everything ordered *just so.*"

"And what do you fear he is ordering?" Phoebe prompted when the girl fell silent.

"His life," came the short answer.

At that, Phoebe couldn't help but smile. "He has passed his thirtieth year, Lucy. He has had the ordering of his life for a very long time, and has managed quite well."

Lucy sniffed. "Quite well to arrange a marriage of convenience for himself?"

"To—" Phoebe broke off. "What do you mean?" she forced out through an uncomfortable catch in her throat.

"Why else should he have visited the Towers at such a time?"

Phoebe stared at her blankly.

"I had hoped—but he has not called upon you, so I must fear the worst." She fixed Phoebe with a look of despair. "I have reason to believe he has gone to make Lady Sophia Langley an offer this morning, and I do not think I can bear the thought of him—Miles, of all people!—wed to such a dull, insipid female."

Twelve

Phoebe's hands, which lay folded in her lap, clenched. "Offer for Lady Sophia?" she managed. "Whatever makes you think that is likely?" She refrained from making the comment that filled her thoughts, that she could think of no lady less likely to inspire Sir Miles Saunderton with love. But if that was not what he wanted . . .

"Something he said to my Aunt Jane this morning." Lucy fixed her with an intent stare. "Do you not mind?"

"Mind?" Phoebe pulled herself back together. "It is none of my concern whom your brother chooses to marry. I feel certain she will make him an admirable wife. She is most biddable, and would never challenge his decisions."

"But that is just the point!" cried Lucy. "She will never argue with him, and he will grow more and more tyrannical as the years pass; and it will be quite dreadful for him."

With that, Phoebe found herself in agreement. And to marry where one did not love— It tore at her heart.

What, she wondered suddenly, might have happened

that night at the Pershings had she encouraged Miles rather than put him off? Would it be she he now approached rather than Lady Sophia? Or did she delude herself? If he wanted peace in his marriage, he had made the right choice. But peace did not necessarily imply happiness.

She closed her eyes as regret, deep and aching, plunged through her. Chances and opportunities. Xanthe had provided them, and Phoebe had thrown them away. She'd come to town to form an eligible alliance, to find love, and she'd been too blind—and too stubborn—to recognize it when it appeared. And now she had nothing, and no hope.

No, that wasn't quite right. She did have something. She had the love that had crept up on her subtly, slowly, filling her until it encompassed her entire being, and she hadn't realized until it was too late. Now it left her desolate.

And what of Miles? Why should he tie himself into this bloodless marriage? Lady Sophia would never love him, never tell him off for his own good, never light that spark of passion in his eyes. And now, neither could she.

Her eyes stung, and she turned her head, blinking rapidly to rid herself of the vexatious tears that threatened. Crying never did any good. But the thought of Miles, dooming himself to so tepid a partner as Lady Sophia Langley, was more than she could bear. He would never know any real happiness with so spiritless a lady. She didn't share his love of music; she never rode in the park in the mornings. He would be so much alone. . . .

Well, there was very little she could do if he had made the irrevocable step of offering for the lady. But what she could do, she would. She could assure he knew some measure of love and companionship. She focused her gaze on Lucy, who sat in silence, watching her with an intensity that surprised her.

"What are you going to do about it?" Lucy demanded.

Phoebe managed a smile. "Give him an engagement present."

"But—you cannot mean you approve of this decision of his!"

"It has nothing to do with me." She kept the bleakness from her voice with a tangible effort. "Are you acquainted with Ashby's cousin, Lady Wrexham?"

"Gussie?" Lucy stared at her as if she had gone mad. "Of course. But whatever—" She broke off as comprehension dawned. "You intend to give him a puppy! But why?"

So that he would have something to love, and something to love him, but she could hardly tell Lucy that. Instead, she returned an evasive answer, which did not satisfy the girl in the least. Nothing would do but that Lucy must accompany her on her errand. To this Phoebe at last acquiesced and sent for the carriage, and less than twenty minutes later they set forth to Mount Street where they were lucky enough to find her ladyship at home.

They were not the only visitors. As the butler ushered them into the elegantly appointed salon, Ashby looked up from where he had gone down on one knee beside the box of growing pups. His gaze fell on Lucy, and Phoebe's heart ached to see the glowing warmth of his expression. If only Miles looked at her like that. But it was too late.

Lucy greeted her hostess, a raven-haired young matron with a laughing eye, very like in appearance and manner to her handsome cousin. Then Ashby called her, and she knelt at his side. He leaned toward her, pointing out the various pups, telling her what they had been about that morning. One he picked up, handing it to her, and as she took it, she raised her gaze to his face with a tremulous smile.

Phoebe felt an aching pull at her heart, and turned to Lady Wrexham. "We have come about a puppy," she said.

Ashby looked up. "Does Lucy wish one?"

"It is for Miles." Lucy hugged the pup and returned it to the box, only to select another.

Gussie Wrexham brightened. "He'll be the perfect home for one of them. It's such a worry, trying to find good homes for all of them, you must know." She looked into the box, considering. "Simon, which do you think he would like? That one?" She pointed to a little male that industriously tried to dig its way out of the far corner.

"How about this one?" He reached in and stroked the back of a sleeping ball of liver-and-white fur. Lucy instantly replaced the one she held and picked that one up instead, receiving a cavernous yawn from it for her efforts.

Phoebe studied each of the pups, looking for she knew not what. One stared back at her with large, soulful brown eyes, and she was lost. She stooped down to pick it up, and its ecstatic tongue went to work first on her hands and arms, then on her chin.

"That's one of the females," Gussie Wrexham said, "and quite my own favorite. No," she laughed as Phoebe started to replace it. "Only look how many I have to settle. I should be delighted for Miles to take her."

"How soon?" asked Phoebe. Now that she held it, she didn't want to put it back.

Lady Wrexham looked to Ashby. "I was going to start letting them go tomorrow," she said after a moment. "One day earlier should make no difference."

Lucy came to inspect Phoebe's selection with delight. "We can take her with us now?"

With this, Lady Wrexham agreed, and Phoebe tightened her hold on the squirming, licking pup. How could so small and young a creature give so much love? She experienced a strong desire to keep it for herself, not to part with it. But Miles's need for it would be great if he allied himself with Lady Sophia.

As great as her own? she wondered, then thrust the thought from her mind. She didn't want to consider the bleakness of her own future at the moment.

They stayed long enough to drink a cup of tea, then took their leave with Phoebe still carrying the puppy. Lucy showed a tendency to linger beside Ashby, who accompanied them down to the waiting barouche. He offered to hold the puppy while Phoebe settled herself, but she refused to part with her squirming burden for even so short a time. Amused, Ashby assisted them in, promised to see them at dinner that evening, and waved the carriage on.

The puppy stood on Phoebe's lap, hanging its little head over the side of the carriage, watching the vehicles and horses and people until, exhausted by so much excitement, it curled up on Phoebe's skirts with a contented sigh and fell asleep. It would be lonely for its littermates that night, Phoebe knew, and sympathized. She herself was likely to be lonely every night for the rest of her life.

"When will you give her to him?" Lucy demanded.

The sooner the better, Phoebe realized. The longer she waited, the harder the parting would be. "Tonight. You are to come to dinner, remember? Or do you think he will be dining with Lady Sophia?" Phoebe stroked the peaceful head, and thought of Miles, asleep from the laudanum. How it must have chafed at his proud spirit to have been so helpless. But, like the puppy, the helpless stage soon passed, and he had made it abundantly clear he had no further need of her.

"He'll come," Lucy declared with a gleam in her eye.

He probably would, she reflected. He was not one to put a hostess out once he had accepted an invitation. And since it would be a very small party, with only Ashby and Mr. Colney invited as well, he would probably announce his engagement. The prospect plunged her into deeper gloom.

Xanthe greeted the advent of a puppy into her household with remarkable aplomb—remarkable, at least, until Phoebe remembered that as a *fairy* godmother, the depredations that so young an animal could make upon her salon need not trouble her in the least. Nor did Titus object. The large, lazy cat eyed the boisterous new arrival, blinked sleepy eyes at it, and the puppy thereafter appeared deferential in the extreme to the massive feline.

When Phoebe finished settling the puppy under Titus's watchful eye in a makeshift pen in the library, she looked up to find Xanthe standing behind her. Phoebe straightened her drooping shoulders, lifted her chin and forced a smile to her lips. "He will like her, will he not?"

Xanthe ignored her question. "You want to keep her yourself."

Phoebe stroked a flopped ear. "I couldn't. When I leave you at the end of the Season, I have no idea where I'll go. No employer would welcome me with a puppy in tow."

"You wished for a husband," Xanthe reminded her.

Phoebe kept her gaze on the spaniel. "And I threw away my opportunity."

"Nonsense. There are several weeks still to go."

A shaky laugh escaped Phoebe. "Oh, dear, I feel like Lucy. I couldn't possibly marry another gentleman when I—when my heart has been given to another."

"Then, you must marry him," came the prompt response.

Phoebe fought back the tears that blinded her eyes. "He doesn't want me."

A sigh escaped Xanthe. "And you think Lady Sophia to be without spirit. I had not thought you would give up so easily."

Phoebe flushed. "What would you have me do? I cannot order a gentleman to desire to marry me."

"You may encourage him to do so."

"It's too late for that." Bleakness crept into her voice.

"It is never too late."

Phoebe shook her head. "If he has offered for her—"

"*If,*" Xanthe said. "It is by no means certain that he has. But it will make no difference at all if you insist on accepting defeat before it is even handed to you. My love, your future is in your own hands now. Magic can do no more for you. Do nothing, and your failure is assured. Act, and you may still win through."

May. Xanthe had not said *will.*

"You have one more opportunity this night," her fairy godmother said softly. "Do not throw it away."

One last opportunity to convince Miles that offering for any other lady than herself would be a dreadful mistake. One last opportunity to win the love she longed for, his love. One last opportunity. . . .

Phoebe spent the remainder of the day with the puppy, playing with it, watching it sleep, deriving what comfort she could from its unquestioning delight in her company. As the hour approached to prepare for their guests' arrival, she considered asking Xanthe for assistance in dressing. But Xanthe had said magic could do no more for her. It was up to her. With this in mind, she donned her favorite of Madame Bernadette's gowns, the one of amber silk and blond lace, and arranged her hair in a becoming style which allowed a cascade of curls to fall around her face. About her neck she clasped a simple gold locket, the only jewelry she possessed that did not owe its existence to Xanthe's humming. With considerable trepidation, she made her way down the stairs to await Miles's arrival.

His manner, when at last he put in his appearance, gave nothing away. He greeted her with a warmth that had been lacking at their last meeting, but Phoebe didn't dare place any hope on that. In fact, now that he was here, she hadn't the faintest idea how she was to broach so intimate a topic as his potential forthcoming marriage. Any hope that Lucy might be of assistance proved futile. Lord Ashby had arrived before her, and as soon as the girl had greeted her hostesses, she went to his side and proceeded to converse with him in an unusually solemn manner.

Which, as Xanthe had warned her it would, left the matter entirely in Phoebe's own hands.

No opportunity for private speech presented itself until after the meal had drawn to an end, and, in the absence of a host, all had retired to the drawing room together. While Mr. Colney, Mrs. Mannering and Xanthe settled around a card table, Lucy drew Ashby into a corner to resume their interrupted conversation. Phoebe found herself facing Miles, and knew her time—and opportunity—had come.

"Has something occurred to trouble you?" he inquired, a slight frown creasing his brow.

Yes! she wanted to cry, but could not. She sought words with which to ask him if all her hopes and dreams were for naught, but none came. At last, she asked him to accompany her to the library, and led the way.

The puppy sprang to its feet the moment she entered the room, pawing at the barrier as it whimpered for attention. Miles went to it at once, picking it up and receiving its frantic licks. Over the top of its head, he asked, "One of Gussie Wrexham's?" He stroked the pup's soft fur. "I've thought of getting one, too."

And there was her opportunity.

She swallowed, very much afraid. In the next few minutes she would know. "This one is for you."

He looked up at that, his brow snapping down. "Why?"

"So you will have something to love." There, she'd said it, she'd actually gotten it out, and there could be no turning back. She'd seized her opportunity, and now she would find out if she were too late.

He regarded her with a slight frown. "I'm afraid I do not understand."

"She is an engagement present," Phoebe declared before her faltering nerve could vanish all together.

"Engagement?" He regarded her from beneath his lowered brow, studying her, his expression giving nothing away. "Somewhat precipitous, perhaps."

"Is it?" She held her breath. If this meant he had not yet offered for Lady Sophia—

"Why," he said softly, "do you think I should need something to love? Especially if I am on the verge of becoming engaged?"

"Then, you haven't offered for her!" Phoebe exclaimed. "Oh, I am so glad. But you mustn't do it." Once started, the words rushed from her. "She wouldn't suit you in the least. She could not possibly love you as much as—" She broke off, stemming the flow just in time.

"Wouldn't she?" He watched her closely, a task

made difficult by the frantically licking tongue that assailed his chin. "Of whom, by the way, are we speaking?"

"Why, Lady Sophia, of course. Lucy said—" She broke off, faltering at his expression of mingled consternation and amusement. "Lucy!" she breathed in dawning horror. "You—you never had any intention whatsoever of offering for Lady Sophia, did you? *Did* you?" she demanded.

"None in the least. We are very old friends, I must admit, but I find I desire a great deal more than that with the lady I marry."

Phoebe drew an unsteady breath. "Lucy is every bit as much a meddler as ever you could be," she declared with savage feeling.

"It seems to run in our family." Very slowly, he closed the distance between them. In one arm he still held the squirming puppy, but his other hand encircled the nape of her neck. "Do you not want to know what it is I desire in marriage?" His fingers strayed along her skin, tickling in the fine hairs that lined her neck.

Phoebe looked down, her heart pounding. "I beg your pardon. I seem to have made a complete fool of myself. And when I see your sister, I shall strangle her."

"Rather extreme, don't you think?" His thumb reached her jaw, stroking it gently, followed by fingers that trailed down her throat. He had begun to smile. "Her meddling was well intentioned, if unnecessary. But then you must remember she had no idea I had matters well in hand. She probably feared I would never get around to it, so she gave you a push." His thumb traced the line of her lower lip, and his hand cupped her chin. "You did imply something about loving me, did you not?"

Her cheeks burned. "I—I was laboring under a misapprehension. And if you were at all a gentleman, you would have the decency to ignore ridiculous statements made when—" She faltered, searching for an explanation that might not sound wholly ridiculous.

"This is one moment when I believe I shall prefer *not* to be a gentleman."

He released her chin, only to encircle her shoulders with his arm and draw her to him. His mouth closed over hers, demanding, both sweet and urgent. She melted against him, clinging to all she thought she had lost. His lips brushed her cheek, found her mouth again, and conscious thought ebbed away.

A protesting yip, followed by a brisk licking of her chin, brought her back to a sense of her surroundings. Miles, chuckling softly, released her and set the pup by the hearth. The look he directed at Phoebe set her pulse racing.

"I've been wanting to do that since that first night I saw you perched on the railing in Queen's Square, trying to reach that windowsill," he informed her.

She swallowed, still finding it difficult to breathe. "I've been wanting you to."

The door opened, and Lucy burst in, dragging Ashby by the hand. "There you are, Miles. Simon has something he particularly wishes to ask you." She thrust her companion forward, then cast Phoebe a sideways, eager glance.

Ashby grinned. "She seems to feel I must ask your formal permission to pay my addresses to her."

Miles's eyebrows rose. "Does she, indeed? Now, why should that surprise me?"

Lucy blushed. "Don't be disagreeable, dear Miles. You know perfectly well you like things done in the proper manner."

"I do, yes. But it comes as a surprise to hear that you do." He turned to Ashby. "Is she suitably aware of the honor you do her?"

"Miles!" Lucy protested.

He fixed her with a reproachful look. "My dear girl, you come bursting in here, interrupting me in the middle of an extremely important discussion, just to—"

"Did I?" Her countenance brightened, and she spun to face Phoebe. "Dear Miss Caldicot, pray say you will marry him. It would be the very thing."

Phoebe clasped her hands before her. "I cannot possibly."

Lucy's face fell. "But—"

"He has not asked me."

"Really, Miles." She regarded him in exasperation. "Never did I think you to be such a slowtop. Whatever is keeping you?"

Miles, who had drawn his snuff box from his pocket during this discussion, offered the box to Ashby, then took an infinitesimal pinch himself. "Lack of opportunity."

"Well, of all the ridiculous things to say!" Lucy exclaimed. "When we left you in here until I could not bear the suspense a moment longer. Whatever have you been doing this last half hour and more?"

"Ashby," Miles said, "unless you wish me to forbid the banns, you will oblige me by removing my sister."

Ashby grinned. "Come along, Lucy."

"But, Simon!" Lucy stood her ground. "Only look how much time he has wasted. He will never get around to it if we don't stay here to give him the nudge."

"Ashby?" Miles's voice took on a threatening note.

That gentleman took a firm grip on Lucy's arm and dragged her from the room. At the threshold he turned back. "She has a point, you know," he said, then shut the door before Miles could say anything more.

Miles studied the door for a long minute, as if he expected it to burst open once more. When it did not, he gave a nod of satisfaction and turned back to Phoebe. "Now that we are rid of my tiresome sister, we may finish our discussion."

A soft growl sounded from the floor. Phoebe looked down to see the puppy working industriously on the toe of Miles's evening slipper, his foot still in it. Obligingly, he removed the shoe, handing it over to the delighted animal.

"You should not spoil her," she protested.

"Managing," he murmured. "Besides, I am not spoiling her in the least. I merely wish to preserve my toes. And if you think Vines will ever permit that shoe into his care again after the mauling it has received, you much mistake the matter." He returned to her, placing his hands on her shoulders. "Can you overlook my meddling disposition?"

"It may cause a few arguments," she admitted. "I am not one to be ridden over roughshod."

"As I have already discovered." The smile that lit his hazel eyes brightened. "But I couldn't bear the thought of a wife who gave in to my every unreasonable demand. And Lucy will tell you I'm apt to make many of them."

"I'll keep you reasonable," she promised. "And I shall also demand my own turns at managing."

"Agreed." He drew her close, his mouth once more seeking hers, his arms pressing her tight against him. His lips brushed her eyes, her forehead, then returned to claim her mouth once more.

At last, her head resting against his shoulder, he said, "You needn't worry about your brother. I believe I know of a living that should become available in two or three years. And if that does not work out, there are one or two others—"

A shaky laugh escaped her. "I should have known your family alone could not provide you with sufficient scope for your meddling. Do you manage the affairs of everyone you know, as well?"

"Only of those I love. Which reminds me, I have spent the better part of this week readying the estate for your arrival. I spoke to the vicar, and he has agreed to post the banns this Sunday. Vines has promised to see to the hiring of an abigail for you, and—"

"Managing," she sighed, and stopped him by the simple expedient of dragging his head down so she could kiss him. "And I shall hire my own abigail, thank you."

"Managing," he got out before she kissed him again.

Epilogue

Xanthe sat back from the shallow silver basin, a
fond smile playing about her mouth. Seven white candles flickered before her, encircling the scrying bowl,
reflecting off the water and the images of Phoebe and
Miles, locked securely in one another's arms. Another
satisfactory conclusion.

After a moment she picked up the extinguisher and
doused the flames that had burned bright, sealing her
magic. Phoebe wouldn't need it anymore. The water
rippled; sparkles of light danced into the air. Then the
surface stilled, showing nothing but the mirrored bottom.

She looked at Titus. "I shall miss her."

Titus blinked sleepy eyes.

"You, too? But we mustn't repine. She'll be quite
happy, and with the four children they will have, she'll
be very busy. But as for us, it's almost time to be
thinking of our next task."

A series of staccato sounds emerged from the cat's
throat.

"No, not quite yet. We'll see them safely wed first,
never fear." She mused for a moment, then smiled.

"This has been an unusually productive undertaking even for us, has it not?"

Titus twitched the end of his tail.

"Of course, they might have all sorted out their lives on their own, but I like to think we played some part in it. Hanna Brookstone and Charles Dauntry, Lucilla Saunderton and Simon, Lord Ashby. Even Mrs. Jane Mannering and Mr. Colney will make a match of it within a few more months. And Phoebe and Miles, of course. No wonder it has all been so exhausting."

Titus tilted his head and flicked an ear.

Xanthe looked at the candles she had not yet replaced in their ashwood cask, and shook her head. "I don't think so, not this time. I feel—" She broke off, and came to her feet, then strode to her window. Casting the drapes wide, she looked out into the night. For a long moment she gazed into the midnight sky of deep blue, with its myriad stars and the thinnest crescent of a moon. The stars shimmered, basking her in iridescent light.

Starlight . . .

Smiling, she turned back into the room.

ABOUT THE AUTHOR

Janice Bennett lives with her family in California. She is the author of over ten Zebra Regency romances and is currently working on the second installment of her *Wish* trilogy. Look for the return of Xanthe in *The Starlight Wish,* coming from Zebra Books in November, 1999. Janice loves to hear from readers, and you may write to her c/o Zebra Books. Please include a self-addressed stamped envelope if you wish a response.

BOOK YOUR PLACE ON OUR WEBSITE AND MAKE THE READING CONNECTION!

We've created a customized website just for our very special readers, where you can get the inside scoop on everything that's going on with Zebra, Pinnacle and Kensington books.

When you come online, you'll have the exciting opportunity to:

- View covers of upcoming books
- Read sample chapters
- Learn about our future publishing schedule (listed by publication month *and author*)
- Find out when your favorite authors will be visiting a city near you
- Search for and order backlist books from our online catalog
- Check out author bios and background information
- Send e-mail to your favorite authors
- Meet the Kensington staff online
- Join us in weekly chats with authors, readers and other guests
- Get writing guidelines
- AND MUCH MORE!

Visit our website at
http://www.zebrabooks.com

LOOK FOR THESE REGENCY ROMANCES

SCANDAL'S DAUGHTER   (0-8217-5273-1, $4.50)
by Carola Dunn

A DANGEROUS AFFAIR   (0-8217-5294-4, $4.50)
by Mona Gedney

A SUMMER COURTSHIP   (0-8217-5358-4, $4.50)
by Valerie King

TIME'S TAPESTRY   (0-8217-5381-9, $4.99)
by Joan Overfield

LADY STEPHANIE   (0-8217-5341-X, $4.50)
by Jeanne Savery

ROMANCE FROM JANELLE TAYLOR

ROMANCE FROM FERN MICHAELS

DEAR EMILY   (0-8217-4952-8, $5.99)

WISH LIST   (0-8217-5228-6, $6.99)

AND IN HARDCOVER:

VEGAS RICH   (1-57566-057-1, $25.00)